JAILBREAK

Shiloh was less than fifty yards away when all hell broke loose at the jailhouse. The cursing shouts of thirty drunks with a hanging rope rang in his ear. Then came the shots.

Shiloh did not look back. He dug his boots firmly into his horse's stirrups and pulled down on the reins. There were at least fifteen of them now running across the field. Behind them were four or five riders advancing at full gallop.

As he rounded the corner of the house, Shiloh could hear the posse's bullets shatter windows. They were firing at a gallop, but their aim was good enough. He felt the hot buzz of two streaming bullets at chest level, then another pounding into the saddle.

A dozen more shots sang out from the approaching horsemen. The horse came down slowly under him, back-end first. Turning toward the posse, Shiloh saw the gunman against the moonlight. He was sitting straight up in the saddle on the still horse, rifle raised for another shot.

Shiloh swung his foot from the stirrup as the second shot echoed across the field. The bullet hit him high, up under his left arm, knocking him from the saddle and down the stream bank. . . .

Books in the SHILOH series by Dalton Walker

SHILOH

THE HUNTED

DALTON WALKER

DIAMOND BOOKS, NEW YORK

THE HUNTED

A Diamond Book / published by arrangement with
the author

PRINTING HISTORY
Diamond edition/July 1991

ISBN: 1-55773-544-1

Diamond Books are published by The Berkley Publishing
Group, 200 Madison Avenue, New York, New York 10016.
The name "DIAMOND" and its logo are trademarks
belonging to Charter Communications, Inc.

PRINTED IN THE UNITED STATES OF AMERICA

10 9 8 7 6 5 4 3 2 1

For Melissa Suzanne

She is the jukebox of my heart, the top shelf in the honky-tonk of my mind, and the pint bottle under the front seat of my soul. She has never given me a last call for her love in those dark and thirsty hours.

1

THE LATE AFTERNOON sky was the color of shabby whorehouse sheets. The ground, dry and rocky, passed slowly under the sure steps of his horse. Since leaving town, Shiloh's thoughts had turned from murderous to morose. He hated it all—the tattered grubby sky, the barren half-desert trail, and the sad self-pitying song of his thoughts.

He had everything, yet it felt worse than having nothing at all. Sitting atop a fine bay mare, with new clothes on his back, a shining new Winchester repeater in the boot, and nearly five thousand in gold in his saddlebags, Shiloh felt as poorly as he ever had. The money was a comfort; Lord knows he had seen his share of days without the price of a decent meal. Still, he hated it all.

The bay's high-headed bridle-wise manner seemed too damn fancy. The beast climbed the rocky trail like a goat and acted glad at the chance, which more than likely meant she was a jughead underneath the gleaming coat. That, and the fact that he probably paid too much for her, made Shiloh hate the horse.

Then too, the Winchester's slick walnut finish and the lever's smooth, well-oiled action felt strange to the touch. When he fired the .44-40 behind the gunsmith's, he couldn't hit the sandbag from twenty steps. The gunsmith hadn't been any help, triggering off six rounds in a neat cluster a child could cover with one hand.

"What line of work you say you were in?" the fat gunsmith had asked with open contempt as he stooped to retrieve the spent cartridges.

And there was the money. Earned for a dirty piece of work, it had the blood of six or more men on it—though every saloon keeper, barber, dry goods store, and bath from Gold Hill to Masonic were glad enough to take their piece. The clerks and bar-dogs were like damn birds, pecking and worrying over fresh shit in the road, cheerfully hunting out what precious grain they could find. They all chirped happily, "yes sir-ing" and fetching as fast as they could manage.

And the whores only made it worse, laughing and joking like they did. They sat lightly on Shiloh's lap and curled their fingers through his hair and sniffed at the lilac water the barber had splashed over him. The lilac water had cost a nickel extra, and the whores enjoyed it more than he did. They weren't bashful to say so either, as they urged him up to their rooms and out to the cribs. But what that money bought, be it for three, five, or twenty dollars, brought only the grimmest of comforts and not enough pleasure to mention.

The whores, the store clerks, and bartenders couldn't sell Shiloh what he wanted. He, himself, couldn't put a name to it.

Now he was out on some lonesome trail with a high-bred horse, feeling like a stranger in his own skin.

He was riding low in the hills, the weight of the Sierra Nevadas on one side and the light of a failing sun on the other. As he started west the trail changed from rock and brown grass to sage and juniper. As he continued, these gave way to a scattering of Jeffrey pine that bordered both sides, casting light shadows across the way.

Christian Brady's ranch lay between Copley and Bodie. And if he were lucky, Shiloh would make it there before full dark.

Shiloh didn't know what to expect. He had never been to Brady's spread, never seen the pretty girl he was said to have married, and had only reacquainted himself with Brady recently. Brady was working for the Pinkertons and leading the life of a gentleman rancher.

Shiloh knew that his chances were better than even that Brady would greet him politely enough. He could probably even expect a good night's sleep in the barn and a hot meal. But all the while, there would be the unasked question: "When you pulling out, stranger?" The wife would be asking it before Shiloh stepped down from his horse. It would take Brady an hour or so to get around to thinking it.

"Darling, he's just a fella I soldiered with in the war," Brady would whisper to his wife in bed.

"Chris, how long will he stay?" she would ask.

And the next day, maybe even over breakfast with the wife at the stove, Brady would say it out loud: "Where ya headin' to?" He'd ask it nice and polite, but in just such a way that was sure to send a man out to saddle his horse after the second cup of morning coffee.

This is what Shiloh thought about as he cleared a small rise that overlooked a spread of fine pasture. There wasn't a thought in his head of how to answer Brady. A half dozen dodgers neatly folded in his saddlebags detailed the crimes of wanted men. All of them more dumb than desperate. Together, they wouldn't add up to a third of what Shiloh carried in his saddlebags or give a man a decent reason to track them. To tell Brady that he was on the trail of such men was worse than a lie, it was laughable. It would be better to say that he was just moving on. Chances were good that Brady wouldn't so much as ask the direction.

There was a light now at the far end of the pasture. Shining in the darkening shadows of twilight like a beacon, a single lantern marked the main house of Brady's spread. Shiloh urged the bay forward with a touch of his spurs. The animal broke into a fine canter, coming down from the hills and following the trail easily through the deepening shadows of pine.

Shiloh rode the fence around the pasture's borders and approached the house. A scattering of cattle closest to the wire lifted their heads slowly, as if with much effort, to consider Shiloh with large bored eyes as he passed.

A figure rose from a chair on the house's back porch, took the three steps down to the yard, then waited, hands on hips. Although he was too far off to make out the face, Shiloh could tell it was Brady. He lifted a hand in greeting, and the figure slowly returned the gesture.

Gathering in the reins, Shiloh approached the fenced yard, bringing the bay to an easy walk. Keeping his eyes on Brady's face, he saw a smile spread across the man's regular features. As Brady started across the yard, scattering chickens in his long-strided walk, the back door opened, and a woman's face appeared. She was wiping her hands on the front of a flour-sack apron, her pretty face screwed up into a question.

Brady shouted something over his shoulder, and the woman stepped out onto the porch.

"Well goddamn," Brady said, opening the gate. He was wearing a pair of worn suit trousers and a clean, collarless white shirt. He looked every inch the gentleman rancher. "If it isn't him in the flesh."

Shiloh stepped down from the horse and led it through the open gate by the reins. "Not disturbing anything, am I?"

"Disturbing? Hell no!" Brady said, the smile fading a little from his face as his two dark eyes worked their way over Shiloh. They were the eyes of a lawman and missed nothing.

"Finished a piece of work up north a ways, and figured I'd pay a visit," Shiloh said, falling in step alongside Brady as they walked toward the barn.

"Work is what you call that now?" Brady said, laughing. "Heard about it from some of the company boys who were passing through. Sounded just about nasty enough to be you. Sounded like one helluva thing."

"It was something, Chris," Shiloh replied.

They were at the double doors of the barn now. Above the doors, painted across the weathered gray boards, was a large eye. Shiloh recognized it as the unblinking insignia of the Pinkerton Agency. He had seen enough of them on the company's circulars.

Brady stopped alongside Shiloh to admire his own handiwork. "You like it?" he asked. "I do believe Allan Pinkerton himself would be tickled if he could see it."

"You still working for them folks?" Shiloh asked, already knowing the answer.

"Hell yes," Brady said, moving forward to unlatch the barn doors. "Their money spends as well as anyone's. And they treat me right."

Brady heaped fresh straw into a stall while Shiloh unsaddled the bay. When they had bedded the horse down for the night, they stepped back out through the doors to see the woman standing on the porch. She was surrounded by clucking chickens who waited for a surprise feeding that would never come.

"Amelia," Brady called as they approached the house, "I want you to meet Hank Proffitt, also known as Shiloh."

The woman had come off the porch and was approaching the barn. Her face showed neither pleasure nor annoyance. Her eyes took in Shiloh completely, from his new set of clothes, covered in trail dust, to the tied-down Colt at his leg and the new Winchester he held comfortably in one hand.

Shiloh took off his hat and one glove, then stepped forward to take the woman's extended hand. She wasn't one of those prissy women who nodded and smiled, looking at the ground when they were introduced. She looked Shiloh right in the eye, then reached her hand out real quick, just like a man would.

She was prettier up close. Although nearly thirty, her delicate good looks had not been ruined by ranch work. Her face had a hint of the sun. Her thin blonde hair fell out from the pinned-up pile on her head to frame her large lake-blue eyes. Pushing an errant strand of hair away with one hand, she took Shiloh's hand in the other.

"Pleased to meet you, Mr. Proffitt," she said, her voice small and shy, but her grip surprisingly firm.

"Well goddamn," Brady interrupted. "Don't just stand there holding hands. Let's get some food in this old boy! By the looks of him he hasn't had a decent meal in a year or more. Too damned busy growing up with the country or some damned nonsense."

"I believe there's some chicken left, Mr. Proffitt," she said. "And a piece of ham steak."

"That'll be fine," Brady answered for Shiloh. "And those biscuits, we have a couple of those biscuits left."

The woman hurried ahead of the two men and vanished through the door to the house. Brady watched her with a look not of ownership, but something else. Shiloh took it to be pride, maybe.

"She's a fine woman," Brady said when she was gone through the door. "Spirited as hell and strong willed. Been married going on five years now, and I swear, every day's a surprise."

The look had not faded from Brady's face. Those dark lawman's eyes were still softened, a small smile played around the corners of the stern mouth. Now, Shiloh knew the look wasn't pride either; it was love. "If she puts up with the likes of you, I reckon she's patient too."

"That she is," Brady said, as they climbed the three even stairs to the porch. "Now, you just sit there and rest yourself."

Shiloh took a seat on one of the three rough-hewn chairs and considered the spread. It was a nice place. Though he had expected that. Brady would not live in less. Shiloh looked out over the yard, with its busy chickens, the gray solid barn. Beyond was the fenced pasture, bordered by rich grasslands and peppered with tidytips, Johnny-jump-ups, and baby blue-eyes. The wildflowers seemed to glow blue and gold in the fading sun.

"Pretty, isn't it?" Brady said, planting himself on the chair closest Shiloh.

"About as pretty as I've seen," Shiloh answered.

As he looked back to Brady, he saw the look of schoolboy love had still not faded from his friend's face.

"How many head are you running?" Shiloh asked.

"Not enough to get rich," came the answer, "but enough to stay happy. There's these here, and then I got another ten head out in a south pasture. Pigs are out behind the barn. Didn't want them spoiling the view."

They were quiet for a time after that, long enough for the sun to sink below the jagged edge of the Sierras. Soon, the woman, Amelia, would call them in for the supper she had prepared for Shiloh.

"You going to tell me then or no?" Brady asked.

"Tell you what?" Shiloh asked, still looking out over the darkening pasture.

"You going to tell me why you rode in here with saddlebags so heavy with gold you almost need a mule to pack it?" Brady said, leaning both elbows on his knees and turning to study Shiloh's face. "And looking so damned sad you'd think Jesus didn't love you and your eyes didn't fit."

2

BEFORE SHILOH COULD answer, Brady's wife came through the door and announced that dinner, such as it was, was ready. The yard, the pasture, and the hills were all dark, yet Brady, reluctant to leave what little view was left, rose slowly, hesitantly, from his chair.

The pump was around the side of the porch. Brady fetched some soft flour-sack towels and a chunk of store-bought soap. Shiloh stripped down to the waist and began working the pump. A small bucket sat under the iron spigot and when it was nearly full, Shiloh began to wash. He started on his face, then worked the smooth cloth over his neck and chest. Brady held the lantern for him like a servant. The white cloth with its faded blue lettering came away soiled as Shiloh worked it over his arms and hands.

"You still wearing that damned coat?" Brady said, nodding toward the faded, patched, and frayed Union coat that Shiloh had hung on the pump head.

"It's warm enough, I suppose," Shiloh said, pulling his long underwear up around his shoulders and slipping into the blue cotton shirt he wore.

"I would reckon you wear that thing for a whole bunch of reasons," Brady answered dryly. "But I don't see warmth as any one of them."

They were walking back around the house now. Shiloh had the coat draped over his arm. "I figure maybe I shoulda let go of it a while ago," Shiloh said. He indicated the coat, but both he and Brady knew what he really meant.

"Smartest thing would be to leave it out on the trail someday," Brady said. "But you would have done that years ago, if you took a notion."

Shiloh stopped and turned at the foot of the stairs. "You figure I just plain don't want to," he said.

"Friend, you hold on to all of it, the coat and the rest,'cause you're plain afraid of letting go," Brady answered. The edge to his voice cut through Shiloh as cleanly as a sharp blade. It cut and twisted at him somewhere deep in his gut. "And you can save the rest of what you have to say for the ladies, because I know better."

Shiloh didn't answer Brady; he would think of what his friend said later. Maybe they would discuss it, if they could. Right now, there was a pretty woman in a kitchen waiting on both of them. He turned again, away from Brady and toward the porch, and walked the three stairs to the door.

Shiloh thought how strange it was that he had not washed when he first reached the ranch. It was as if he was waiting to see if he was welcome at this place. And now Shiloh knew that he surely was. There had been surprise in Brady's manner, but none of the awkward silences of forced hospitality. Brady and the woman, Amelia, had welcomed him into their home, without questions or hesitation.

"You think about what I said," Brady whispered at Shiloh as they entered the kitchen. "You think on it real good."

The most startling thing about the kitchen was the stove. Shiloh would have expected, if he had thought of it, a small Prairie Queen or some such. Instead, he was greeted by an immense iron and enameled thing that took up nearly an entire wall of the small kitchen. It was perhaps the largest stove Shiloh had ever seen. The white enameled surface boasted pictures of flowers across the three large doors, at the top, and on its sides. It required three stovepipes and looked as if it could accommodate and burn a cord of hickory in one using.

"It's a beaut, ain't it?" Brady asked, perhaps mistaking Shiloh's wide-eyed stare of astonishment for one of admiration.

"Can't say that I've ever seen one like it," Shiloh replied, approaching the stove. The whole chicken that the woman pulled from one of its ovens looked no bigger than a sparrow as it emerged from the cavernous device.

"Not likely to see one like this any time soon, either," Brady said, proudly. "Had her brought in all the way from Sacramento. Found her in a hotel and bought her up."

"Now, Chris, don't go bragging on the stove again," Amelia cautioned. "Though it is a pleasure having enough room when canning season comes around."

"Looks foreign," Shiloh said, stepping around to look at the beast from a sideways angle.

"All the way from Germany the man said," Brady answered. "Brought her out in a Washoe wagon, not a scratch on her."

"And I never heard such cursing and yelling," Amelia put in, as she set the chicken down on the table. "Enough to curdle milk. Chris and the driver worked half a day to get the thing off the wagon. Then two days moving it into the house. Chris took it apart piece by piece. We were cooking over a fire in the yard until he figured out how to get it together again inside the house. Mr. Proffitt, your dinner is ready for eating."

Shiloh took a seat at the table in front of the chicken. From another door on the stove's ornate front, the woman pulled a thick slice of cured ham. And from still another, a heaping basket of fresh biscuits.

Shiloh began to eat, but before the first forkful was up to his mouth, the woman cleared her throat. When Brady cleared his in response, Shiloh looked up.

The woman was standing on the other side of the table, behind where Brady sat. She was frowning. "Mr. Proffitt, do they say grace where you're from?" she asked.

"I reckon they do, ma'am," Shiloh replied, trying to think back to the last time he had said grace.

"Well then, get on with it," Amelia said.

"Amelia, we ain't eating, he is," Brady said. "If he ain't accustomed to it, you can't make him."

"I most certainly can," she said, her voice as solid and unbending as one of the doors on the huge oven. "In my kitchen, we thank the Lord for his bounty. It needn't be out loud, Mr. Proffitt, the good Lord will hear it in a whisper."

Shiloh didn't answer. Rather, he laid his fork neatly across the plate, folded his hands in his lap, and bowed his head. At first, he was merely going to mumble some words, maybe even one of them would be "bless." But when he closed his eyes the words just came out from his lips in a low whisper. "Lord," he began, "bless this food, but mostly bless this house and these folks. They are fine people and deserve whatever grace you can see fit to give them."

The room fell silent then. So quiet that Shiloh could hear some of the grease from the ham steak sizzle in the pan the woman left on the stove.

It was Brady who finally talked first. "I seen it and I kinda heard it, but I don't believe it," he said. "Shiloh saying grace at the table. If Amelia can do that, then I don't feel so bad about how she got me to marry her. That was a trifling, compared to what I just saw."

"Now, you hush," the woman said. "Let this poor boy enjoy his food in peace."

She was sitting at the table now; Shiloh liked that. He liked the way she just sat down with the men. Most women would have either busied themselves rattling pots and splashing water or left the room the minute food was on the table. This one just sat down.

"No reason you can't listen and eat at the same time, is there?" Brady asked Shiloh. But he didn't wait for an answer, seeing that Shiloh was already cutting large portions of white meat from the chicken and forking them into his mouth. He had never had finer, not even in those fancy San Francisco hotels. It tasted better than any chicken had a right to taste.

Brady continued, "I was out here on assignment for the Pinkertons, and I met this old horse trader. He was god fearing and about as smart as a tree full of owls. And crafty, too. The old cuss could sell ice in winter, and make you wait in line for it."

"Chris, that's my papa you're talkin' about," the woman said. "And he is no horse trader, Mr. Proffitt. He is a preacher by temperament and inclination. We only kept a few horses because he loved them so."

"Maybe so, but if that old man ever ran into the devil, he'd trade him his pitchfork for a swaybacked tobiano," Brady replied with a smile. "Anyway, when my horse pulled up lame, I went to see him. And by the time we made a bargain for this little sorrel, what he didn't know about me wasn't worth knowing."

Shiloh nodded politely with a mouth full of food, to show he was still listening.

"So, when he suggests that we seal the deal with a drink, I don't stop him," Brady continued. "And before long, we're both on the outside of one bottle and working on getting another inside us."

Shiloh could see what was coming, but he let Brady go on.

"Then it gets to be around suppertime," Brady said. "And the old man asked me to stay on. Says he's just a poor widower, but he's got this sort of old-maid daughter, who's a pretty fair hand in the kitchen—"

"Chris!" Amelia cut in, laughing. "It just gets worse with each telling."

Brady smiled a little wider, but pretended to pay her no mind. "So Amelia here, she puts out a spread, the likes of which Vanderbilt himself never saw," Brady said. "And the whole time, the old coot's saying maybe the grub ain't so bad, but it ain't good neither. And about how no woman's cooking is any good until she gets a regular man or husband to cook for, then it just gets better every time she puts food over the fire."

Shiloh split one of the biscuits in two and was rewarded by a sweet buttery cloud of steam. He used this to soak up the ham gravy on his plate.

Brady continued with his story. "There I am, eating every last thing put in front of me and saying how damned good it is. Between the old man's liquor and Amelia's cooking, the next thing I know is I'm standing in a church social, fetching her punch, meeting the ladies' guild, and chatting with the cattlemen's association."

"You were very sweet," Amelia said shyly from across the table. "I was never courted so sweetly."

"And I didn't even know I was courting you!" Brady laughed. "I just know I'm burning up the telegraph wire, making excuses to the Pinkertons about why I'm staying on so long. Then the old boy took me out to this place. And when we got back to town, I sent them a telegraph saying I was getting married."

"Mr. Proffitt," the woman then asked, "what line did you say you were in?"

Shiloh was about to answer, but Brady spoke first. "He's what they call a bounty hunter, Amelia. About the best there is."

The woman didn't seemed shocked; she just sat there with a little smile on her face. The smile could have meant anything. When she spoke again, it was with a clear direct voice. "And you know Chris from the Pinkerton Agency?"

"I met him in the war," Shiloh answered, finishing the last of the ham steak and laying his knife and fork down. "We met in Tennessee."

Her eyes brightened at this. "Then you were there with Chris," she said in a gentle whisper. "I should have guessed, by the name, but I thought it was from the Bible."

"I suppose it was, back a ways," Shiloh answered. Talk of the war had set his heart to pounding. The food he had just eaten felt suddenly heavy in his stomach. "I suppose that's where I first heard of it. 'And the whole congregation of the children of Israel assembled together at Shiloh, and set up the tabernacle of the congregation there. And the land was subdued before them.'" He had no trouble remembering that Bible passage. He had read it a hundred times or more.

The woman scrunched her forehead up prettily. "Isn't that where the Israelites kept the ark?"

"'Let us fetch the ark of the covenant of the Lord out of Shiloh unto us,'" Brady said flatly. His head was bent toward the smooth surface of the table, though he didn't have to strain to remember his Bible. "' . . . that when it cometh among us, it may save us out of the hand of our enemies.'"

A small grim smile of understanding passed between the two men. Both had looked for their own answers between Joshua and Samuel, and beyond those chapters as well. Shiloh had not found his answers, and Brady found only comfort.

"That's right," the woman said, pleased at her husband's reciting. "They took the Lord's word out of the tabernacle into the war—" She cut herself off suddenly then, realizing what she had said. Then she turned from Brady to Shiloh, a look of infinite compassion etched over her face. It was then that she remembered that the war, more than ten years in the past, was never very far from the thoughts of these two men.

"' . . . they fled, every man into his tent,'" Brady whispered, his voice sounding very loud in the quiet room. "'And there was a very great slaughter, for there fell thirty thousand footmen.'"

3

THEY WERE SITTING in the front part of the house. Brady and Shiloh worked away on a matched pair of rocking chairs, taking their time with a bottle of whiskey. After every fourth or fifth sip from the bottle, Brady would rise from his chair and either poke at the small hearth's fire or feed it another pine log, depending on his mood as much as what was required. He wasn't talking or drinking like a man accustomed to getting out from under the covers early in the morning.

Amelia was on a straight-back chair, tending to her sewing. Her small fingers moved with a swift deftness as she guided the needle, first about the cuff of a shirt, then through the nearly new material of a yellow dress. She had not spoken since the Bible quoting during dinner. Now, she spoke with a strong, determined voice. "Mr. Proffitt, I simply do not believe you for an instant," Amelia said, looking only briefly up from her needlework.

Shiloh and Brady looked up at her. "What would that be, Amelia?" Brady asked, lazily tilting a generous portion of whiskey into his mouth, then setting the bottle down between the two rocking chairs.

"I don't believe that either of you're Bible quoting," she said. "Listening to the both of you, a person would think you don't believe that it was a rightful war."

"Now, Amelia, don't go on about what you don't know," Brady said. His voice was not stern, but it was serious. It was a warning. Shiloh imagined that Brady didn't talk much of the war, even with Amelia.

"I know the Lord's word well enough," she said, through tight lips. "I know you, Christian Brady. And I know that war, terrible as it was—"

Brady cut her off before she had the chance to finish. "Just don't go on, Amelia, because you don't know. You may think you do, but you surely don't."

"I have eyes, I can see," she said tartly. "And I have a brain in my head, thank you. You can talk all you want, but I know what I know."

"And sometimes, Amelia, that isn't a whole lot," Brady shot back.

Shiloh felt his chest swell then tighten with mention of the war and what must surely be an impending argument. Somehow, he had brought ill will into this house. He had ridden in from the trail, and these people had welcomed him. They had been happy before seeing his face at their table; now they were beginning to bicker.

"She maybe isn't wrong, Chris," Shiloh said. "Whatever she says probably isn't wrong."

Both Brady and Amelia looked over at Shiloh, silent, as if expecting some great truth. At that moment, Shiloh felt that it was as if they were both looking down a deep well for their reflections or a patch of sky.

"What are you saying, friend?" Brady asked. "Are you saying that all of that, that it was right?"

"She says it was right," Shiloh replied slowly. "All those people back East say it was. If I don't think too hard on it, sometimes I think it was. And when both of us are long dead, folks will still be saying it was, at least the Union ones will be."

"Saying something don't make it so," Brady said bitterly. Clearly he didn't like what Shiloh had to say. "You were there, I know you didn't think it was right then."

Shiloh took the bottle and drank deeply before answering. "I didn't think much of anything was right and maybe I still don't," he said. Shiloh was talking slowly; he had thought these things before, but this was the first time he tried to say them out loud. "Before it all started, we thought it was right. But we were young and didn't know anything."

"We were young," Brady repeated, taking the bottle from Shiloh.

"Then when it happened, it was wrong," Shiloh said. "We all knew it, nothing that damned bad could be rightful or good. Nothing could. But it's all over now, a bunch of years have gone by and it still seems real close, but it isn't."

"You're leading and I'm following," Brady said, "but I don't know where in hell we're going."

Shiloh took a deep breath; he didn't know either. Suddenly everything he had thought to say vanished. He was trying to puzzle it out as he talked. "Maybe you have to cut out that middle part, so you just remember the before and after. Then you see it like other folks. And then it's right."

Brady frowned deeply. "Is that what you've done?" he asked, his voice that of a man waiting to hear a lie.

Shiloh wanted to tell him about the dead that plagued his sleep and the way his dreams would never let him put it in the past. Thousands of miles and more than ten years had not put enough distance between him and those bad days in Tennessee.

"I can see plain as day, that's exactly what you've done," Brady said. He was nearly yelling now as he leaned across his chair so that his face was inches from Shiloh. "Hell, I can see that, you wearing that Union coat and that cut-away army holster. You've worked real hard at it, haven't you?"

"Christian Brady!" Amelia barked. "That's quite enough! This man's our guest."

Brady turned to his wife, a crooked, nasty grin on his face. "And maybe while you're talking so high and mighty, quoting scripture and such, maybe you want to tell Amelia here about how you've been sleeping for the last ten years or more? Frightening whores and horses with your shouting and whimpering dreams."

"That's enough, Christian!" Amelia barked, lowering the needle and a length of material to her lap.

Brady took another quick drink from the bottle. "No, Amelia, that isn't enough," he spat back at her. "I heard about that old girl in Gold Hill you almost shot. Waking up in a sweat, crying like a baby with that Colt in your hand. You had it cocked, didn't you, thinking she was a butternut?"

Shiloh didn't answer; he could feel himself begin to tremble with shame.

"Hell, I'll tell you how much you put it away," Brady continued. "You can't even talk to folks without them reminding you of it, can you, Shiloh?"

"I don't know," Shiloh whispered. "I can't. It just plain doesn't seem right to forget them. Maybe when we're all dead, maybe that'll put it right."

"Damn, I know you," Brady said, falling back into his chair. He spoke quietly now, like a man who had just lost a fight. "Just like I know myself. There isn't a day I don't think of it. Not a blessed day."

Shiloh watched Brady's face carefully. He wasn't exactly crying, but his eyes were getting wet. Years of holding back what he felt, keeping it cinched down tight, was leaking out. "I just don't know anymore," Shiloh said. "Just give me one little thing to believe. A scrap of something that would set it right."

"There isn't any putting it right," Brady said softly, almost in a whisper. "All the ones that died, they're still dead. They're dead today, and they'll be dead tomorrow."

"That's a truth," Shiloh said, taking a sip from his whiskey.

"And, I can tell you something else," Brady put in. "They're gonna be dead long after we join them. If you want to make peace with them, you're gonna have plenty of opportunity. Me, I just want to make peace with myself."

Shiloh could remember the first time he saw Brady. It was after the killing. Shiloh was digging the graves. Men were lined up on either side of a fifty-foot trench, working away at the heavy clay. Between the rain and the bone-tiredness, the burden was nearly unbearable. But it was almost honest, everyday work. Shiloh's hands had already begun to blister and bleed, yet he kept at it. He spoke to no one, not even the officers who rode by grim-faced on their horses.

Brady was driving a six-mule team, the wagon piled high with bodies. His uniform was in tatters, his arm a bloodied mess from a load of grapeshot.

When he pulled the wagon up near the grave, Shiloh lifted his head from the work long enough to see the dead, stacked like wood under a filthy canvas covering. Some of the flesh was white, where Shiloh could make it out between the slats in the wagon.

Other sections revealed blue arms and torsos, where the blood had gathered after death. Some of the bodies were still streaked with blood or mud; wounds of all description could be seen among the pile of lifeless flesh. Many of the bodies were already blackened and bloated. Some of those on burial detail would stab these with bayonets—releasing a foul stench—before unloading them.

Here and there an open-eyed face pressed against the rough wood.

Shiloh knew the corpses had been loaded carelessly into the wagon's bed, heaved by two men from the ground. When the pile grew too high for this, one man was required to stand on those already loaded and pull the new additions into the wagon. Often limbs—arms, legs, hands—that had been torn by grapeshot or minies fell away from their owners, never to be reunited.

"These came from three miles away," Brady said, climbing down from the wagon. Shiloh noticed that the wounded arm didn't hamper his movements much. He swung down from the wagon in a graceful motion, landing lightly on his feet.

"Union or reb?" someone down the line called, though patches of gray uniform were clearly visible in many places.

"These here are butternut," Brady answered. He was standing beside Shiloh now, examining the trench that would serve as a grave.

"Lord, there's so many of them," Shiloh said. It was the first time he had spoken in two days, his voice raspy with the effort.

"That there is, friend," Brady replied. He looked not toward the wagon, but swept his eyes down the line of the trench and across the field where hundreds of men worked with pick and shovel digging the graves and where a dozen wagons or more unloaded their cargo of the dead.

"Ya can forget 'bout him," someone down the line called to Brady. "He doan talk."

"He just did," Brady replied. "You can talk, can't you?"

Without answering Shiloh turned back to his digging. It would be the last day of the work, and he was anxious to be done with it. The smell of dead men, horses, and mules filled the air. Many of the men worked with neckerchiefs tied over their mouths and noses to guard against the stench, but this did little good.

"Hell, he can talk," Brady tried again. "He's just a hard worker is all."

"He ain't right," a voice down the line said. "He went funny from it."

Shiloh stepped farther down into the trench and sunk his shovel deep into the heavy clay. The work felt good. It made his shoulders and arms burn with the effort. He knew that if he just thought about the work, he wouldn't see the rest of it; not until it was time to lay the bodies down. That was the worst part, laying them down. When they started, he had tried to close all their eyes and lay their hands neatly across their chests. Now, he no longer bothered. Like the rest, he shoveled the heavy dirt into their unseeing eyes, across their still chests, and over the ruined uniforms.

"Nothing wrong with him that a little Cincinnati whiskey can't cure," Brady said, his voice strained for good humor. "Isn't that right, friend?"

Shiloh looked up from his work to the voice. He had not actually noticed Brady before. Now, from the bottom of the trench, he could see his face. The white skin, smudged with smoke and mud, framed by dark hair. The two dark eyes sunk deep. He was only a few years older than Shiloh, yet at that age, a few years meant more than it would later on.

Reaching into a breast pocket, Brady fished out a pint bottle of whiskey and offered it to Shiloh. "This here is Christian Brady buying you this drink," he said.

Shiloh just stared up from the trench. Brady wiggled the half-full bottle some, the brown liquor splashing up into its neck.

"Hell, better offer it to a livin' man," a voice called close by. "That boy ain't done but one thing, from dark to dark, and that's dig holes for butternuts. Seems to prefer dead rebs better'n us."

Shiloh never knew what brought Brady to his side. And he would never question what made Brady step down into the grave alongside him and offer him that bottle of whiskey. He seemed to fear nothing, not the dead he hauled in the wagon, nor the wrath of officers who might see the illicit liquor.

"Now you drink this, friend," Brady said, holding the bottle out.

Shiloh didn't answer. He would remember for a long time what it felt like down in that grave. Brady with his bottle, the men working at his side, the noise of horses straining across the muddied ground, and the distant shouts of men; they all seemed impossibly remote. It was as if it were all a strange language. Everything seemed like a year-old newspaper from a far-off town.

"Why you bothering with him?" a voice sounded close by. "He ain't no good to nobody, 'cept dead rebs."

Shiloh lifted his head from the work to see Brady turn slowly toward the man. He was a private from a Nebraska division.

"He's the man that's gonna help me unload," Brady answered. And then to Shiloh, "Isn't that right?"

Shiloh again looked up from his work. The trench was nearly completed. Four feet deep is what the officers said to dig, and four feet they had dug. The chest-high grave, dug into the heavy clay, would hold fifty or more.

"Isn't that right," Brady said jovially, forcing his face into a smile. Then in a whisper meant only for Shiloh, he said, "You did a fine job, but what's a grave without bodies to fill it? Finish the job and be done with it."

"Lord, but there were so many of them," Shiloh said at last.

Brady stared thoughtfully at Shiloh, taking his time about it. "That there were," he finally answered.

It had been a long time since Brady had risen from the rocking chair to tend the fire. It burned low in the small fireplace. The sweet-smelling pine logs had collapsed in the irons and turned to white ash, but warmth continued from a glowing center.

Shiloh picked up the bottle and looked over to the woman. She had not spoken for a long time. Some women, he knew, were quiet. They wouldn't so much as open their mouths if two men were speaking, but not this one. Amelia spoke her mind, and Shiloh liked that. He wanted now to hear her voice again, as if it could banish his thoughts of death and war.

"I best be off to bed," she said, as if obliging Shiloh's unspoken request. "Some of us in this house rise early." And with that, she carefully stacked the last of her sewing in the basket and rose. "Christian, don't keep our guest up too long. He's had a long day I expect."

And then she was gone, vanished through a door at the opposite side of the room.

"She's a fine woman," Shiloh said, when she left the room.

Brady didn't answer directly; rather, he unfolded himself from the chair lazily, stepped over to the small pile of pine, and casually placed two more wrist-thick logs on the fire. "Now that you've made your fortune," he said, sitting himself back down. "How do you figure on spending it?"

"Haven't given it much thought," Shiloh said, glad to bring the conversation back from the war.

"I can tell you about a small spread a little ways from here," Brady said, smiling, "almost as pretty as this one, where you can run as many or as few head as you want. Good water, a nice orchard, and a pretty little widow woman goes with it."

"You thought this up all by yourself?" Shiloh asked. "Or did Amelia help you some?"

"Hell, you know the story." Brady chuckled. "As long as there's one unmarried man left wandering around pitiful and lonesome, no married woman rests easy."

"I'd say it's more like one unmarried woman that does it," Shiloh said, taking a drink.

"You're not put out, me bringing it up?" Brady asked, his voice genuinely concerned. "It was just something Amelia mentioned, real quick like."

"No, I'm not put out," Shiloh replied heavily. "I was just thinking. You know, I can't remember the last time I had a woman I didn't pay for."

4

SHILOH SLEPT ON the parlor floor in front of the hearth. The clean-swept floor suited him fine. He had gone out to the barn, lantern in hand, to fetch his bedroll, then returned for the night to bed down. Brady had hauled out a new quilt and a fat pillow, for which Shiloh was grateful.

He fell asleep with the fire stoked against the night chill. As he rested back in his bedroll, the pillow under his head and the bottle within easy reach, Shiloh thought again of how good these people had been to him.

Even Amelia had welcomed him into her home. He was a friend of Christian's and that was enough. Shiloh had no doubt she would make up her own mind about him, that would be her way. But she had shown him every kindness.

Then too, it was a pure joy to see Brady again. The last time Shiloh had seen him was out in some dusty town, and Brady was working for the Pinks. In this place, Shiloh could see the real man and not the Pinkerton agent.

As Shiloh dozed near the fire, the whiskey singing sweet and lovely in his brain, he thought on how little Brady had changed. He had grown older, yes, that was to be expected. The thin face with its hard angles and sharp lines had gone a little plump, smoothed over by age and increased no doubt by home cooking. Gray had crept into the thick black hair. Not enough gray to mention, really, just a few iron-colored strands. In a few years he would look distinguished enough to get himself elected mayor.

But Brady's eyes were the same, dark and full of mischief. They were the eyes that were lit with the boyish charm. Brady's eyes, and his quick irascible smile, revealed without shame the secret boy that lives in every man.

When Shiloh fell into sleep, the familiar terror of his dreams did not find him. He dreamed of the war, for it was never far from his mind, but there was no fear in it. And even in his dream he knew this to be a strange and wonderful thing.

He dreamed of a young Christian Brady. They're drinking whiskey by the side of the grave. It is late afternoon, with a spring chill to the air. They're passing the small bottle back and forth without talking. Then Brady takes a final pull on the bottle and slams the cork back in, using the fingers of his good hand. And Shiloh remembers thinking that even with his arm in a sling, he's making out pretty good.

"It's time we get to it," Brady says, tucking the bottle back into his pocket.

Shiloh doesn't answer; rather, he follows this strange, wounded man to the back end of the mule-drawn wagon. Unfastening the canvas covering, Brady throws it back to reveal a half dozen grim and bloated faces staring sightless through the wagon's back slats.

"Lord, but there's so many of them," Shiloh had said. And now he repeats it in his dream.

Shiloh can see that the grave is finished. The men have climbed out and are watching. They lean on shovels and picks. Some are smoking; others are waiting for the water that a boy is offering up from a jug.

"Nothing but a small piece of work for two fit men," Brady says. And with that he climbs up into the wagon with the dead. He steps lightly among the lifeless bodies. They smell as bad as sin, but neither Brady nor Shiloh cover their noses or mouths. One by one they lower the bodies from the cart. At first they try grabbing hold of the torn and blood-hardened cloth of a uniform, but the material rips away in their hands. When this happens, the corpse falls heavily to the ground or against the wagon's lowered gate.

Some of the bodies are clothed in Union uniforms and Shiloh knows these were looted after the first skirmishes. These are the men who marched into the slaughter in rags. They carried little ammunition, many were without even a rifle.

Brady and Shiloh work steadily, laying the bodies out in a neat line beside the trench. Across the field another six-mule team wagon is being worked, its wheels on either side of the grave. A lieutenant is urging the mules on with a whip and curses, while two enlisted men kick and roll butternut corpses off the back end and into the grave. But Brady and Shiloh treat these men gently. It seems important, despite the stares and curses from the men on either side of the trench.

On the first day of burial detail the orders were to lay the bodies neatly in the ground, arms across each man's chest. But as the press to bury the dead became more urgent, bodies were stacked two and three deep, head to toe and crossways, more careless than wood.

When Brady and Shiloh finish the hateful work, a young officer in a crisp uniform rides up. No salute greets him as he orders the others to place the bodies in the trench.

They are both sweating freely now, their woolen uniforms soaked through with it. They wash at the water bucket Brady has fastened to the wagon. He has produced a small bar of lye soap from his coat pocket, and it's with this that they remove the stench and filth of the dead from their hands.

Later, sitting on the moist ground beside the wagon, Brady once again produces the whiskey, but does not pass it.

"This here is now for medicinal purposes," he explains, painfully slipping his arm from the sling.

And it is exactly as Shiloh remembers. Brady strips down the torn uniform and checks the bandages. Fresh blood has soaked through the material, but this only makes Brady smile.

"Should see someone about that," Shiloh says.

Brady looks up with a tight-lipped smirk. "I wouldn't trust those army butchers with a sick dog," he answers, untying the bandage. "My arm would've been on a stack in front of some surgeon's tent by now if I trusted them."

Shiloh doesn't doubt it for a second. He has seen the stacks of arms, legs, and hands, some almost as tall as a grown man. He watches as a portion of Brady's wounded arm is revealed. "Looks bad," he says grimly.

"Ain't so bad some army butcher has to take a saw to it," Brady says, without lifting his eyes from the task.

When the wound is completely exposed, Shiloh can see it. A deep gouge of flesh has been scooped from the upper arm where the minie ball has been dug out, probably by Brady and probably with a pocketknife. A dozen or more maggots have infested the deep wound.

Shiloh recoils in disgust at the sight of the fat white worms writhing blindly in the bright red hole of torn flesh. Blood oozes from the side as the pale worms feast. Brady starts slightly at the sight, his head twisting back as if to disown the maggoty arm.

Shiloh can feel himself moving back against the hard wood of the wagon's wheel at the sight. His mouth fills with bitter bile.

But now Brady is smiling and craning his head closer to the wound, which is nearly completely filled with the vile white worms. "Don't you worry about them," Brady says, grinning up from the sight. "They're nothing but beautiful."

Shiloh knows then that he is in the company of a madman. He's stunned, but he can't take his eyes from the repulsive vision. Even now, in his dream, he feels his stomach churn and tense.

"Friend," Brady says, "I'm gonna need some help here."

And Shiloh helps him. One by one, he picks out the filthy maggots from the wound. Some have burrowed deep, so deep he needs to pry two fingers into Brady's flesh. One he picks out with a clean knife blade. When he is finished, the wound is pink and new, the blood bright.

"Now this is the hard part," Brady says, lifting the bottle of whiskey. "Hard for both of us 'cause we're not drinking good whiskey, but worse for me 'cause it's gonna hurt like sin."

Lifting the bottle, Shiloh prepares to douse the wound. Brady positions himself at the wheel, two hands behind him clenched around the spokes. "No matter what I say," Brady instructs, "you pour most of it on. Just save enough for one drink each."

Shiloh nods and begins pouring. With the first touch of the liquor, Brady kicks and curses, his face going bright red, then white. When Shiloh's finished, he hands the bottle to Brady, who drains all but a few drops before handing it back.

Then they bandage the wound with fresh material. Later, Brady would explain how he became infected and exposed the open gash to attract flies. The maggots, he said, ate out the poison. They turned gray-green flesh pink and brought forth bright red blood where the yellow putrid pus of decay had begun.

"It wasn't pretty," Brady said, when the wound was rebandaged. "And it wasn't any fun. Sometimes you just need some bad to drive out the worse."

Brady kept the wound opened for two more days, to be certain that Shiloh had found all of the maggots, then he talked one of the volunteer aid women into sewing it up with silk thread. Later, Brady would claim that he chose the woman by asking who was the best quilter.

Shiloh awakened to the smell of frying bacon. It called him from the dream. Then he could feel and hear light footsteps through the floor. When he heard the humming, he knew it was Amelia. She was in the kitchen cooking breakfast.

Opening one eye, Shiloh could see that the fire had burned out. Two ends of a log lay on either end of the irons, unburned. Sunlight fell through the two front windows, sending long lines of white light streaking over the smooth floor.

Shiloh rose as quietly as he could, pulling himself out from under the bedroll. Making his way across the room, he stood quietly for a moment a little ways back from the kitchen's doorway. The bacon was sizzling loudly on the stove, and Amelia did not hear him.

But the sight of her made his heart ache. She was standing at the stove in a blue and yellow dress with a flour-sack apron tied around, tending to the bacon. And she was humming to herself, just loud enough to hear.

Shiloh thought to himself that to wake everyday to a woman cooking and humming in a kitchen would be a lovely thing. To roll sleepily over in a warm bed in the morning and know there was a woman cooking for you would be a joy. Even to wake early and cook for that woman would be a pleasure.

Amelia turned suddenly from the stove. The small private smile vanished as her mouth came open in surprise, only to be replaced by a larger, white-toothed smile. "Mr. Proffitt," she said, with a giggle, "you startled me. Breakfast will be ready in a minute. Chris, as usual, is still asleep."

Shiloh took his time in speaking, trying to figure the best way to say it and finally deciding just to say it. "Chris said something about a widow lady?"

This took Amelia completely off guard. Her eyes crinkled slightly around the edges in a determined challenge. "Mr. Proffitt, I don't know what Chris has been telling you, but she isn't like that. Not at all. If you want that sort of thing—"

"He also said something about an orchard," Shiloh tried. "They wouldn't be apples trees?"

"I believe there are some apples," came the answer. "Mostly peach. They say she cans the best peaches in the state." Amelia was smiling. She was smiling so wide and happy it looked as if she was about to bust out laughing.

Shiloh watched her smile and then realized that he was smiling as well.

5

SHILOH WAS HALFWAY through eating when he noticed that Brady was staring at him. A full plate of food and a steaming cup of black coffee sat in front of Brady untouched. He was resting his head on one arm, watching Shiloh eat as if it were the most interesting thing in the world.

"Chris," Amelia said finally, "what's wrong? My cooking doesn't suit you anymore?"

"Food's fine," came Brady's reply. "I just want to know how you did it."

"Cooked it same as any other morning," Amelia said, through a wide smile.

"I want to know how you talked him into it," Brady said, turning from watching Shiloh scrape egg yoke onto a piece of torn biscuit, to his wife.

"I declare, Chris," Amelia said as she reached out for a biscuit off the serving plate. She was still full of good humor and obviously enjoying her husband's consternation. "The world doesn't go exactly like you expect and suddenly you think I'm casting spells in my kitchen."

They were talking as if Shiloh wasn't there, but he had heard every word. And it was true, she had been casting spells, just as surely as an Indian shaman. And Shiloh had seen her, mixing up her secret portions of flour, eggs, water, and soda. He had seen her working and fussing over the crackling bacon and lightly moving around the familiar kitchen in practiced, easy steps. But it wouldn't have worked without the humming.

"You don't have to meet her if you don't want," Brady said, turning to Shiloh. "If you plan on seeing her because you think you have to, well that ain't so."

Shiloh popped the last piece of egg-soaked biscuit into his mouth before answering. "I want to, Chris."

"Well damn," Brady said, getting up from the table. "There's no telling what a man's gonna find when he gets up in the morning, anymore."

"You leaving, Chris?" Amelia said sweetly, rising to retrieve Brady's uneaten breakfast. She could barely contain her pleasure in the face of Brady's confusion.

"I might as well go around the barn and check on the pigs," he replied. "Hell, they might've grown wings last night and are flying around like sparrows. I wouldn't be surprised if it happened, not on the same day Shiloh goes courting."

When Brady was out the door the room fell into a near complete silence. From beyond the porch, the chickens could be heard clucking and scratching. Then, neither Amelia nor Shiloh could contain themselves. They began laughing. It was a laugh that worked its way up from deep down in Shiloh's gut. It made his chest heave and his face spread into an idiot grin. And it was the first time he could remember laughing in a long, long time.

Shiloh and Amelia stopped laughing several times, but each time they tried to wipe the grins from their faces the laughter began anew.

It was Amelia who finally stopped first. She looked across the table at Shiloh with those steady, serious blue eyes and wrinkled her brow prettily. "Why now, Mr. Proffitt?" she asked. "Why take a notion to get married now?"

"Seems about right," Shiloh said, not wanting to tell the full reason. "Why does anyone settle down?"

"I'm afraid that isn't good enough, Mr. Proffitt, not nearly so."

"I guess a man just gets tired," Shiloh said.

"A man can get tired of marriage too," she answered tartly.

"It isn't like that," Shiloh said. "And it isn't easy to talk of."

"Why don't you try," she replied gently. "Chris seems to think it's quite a change of mind, you wanting to go courting."

Shiloh thought for a long moment before answering. He wanted it to come from his mouth just right. "It's like this," he said at last. "You start to get tired. And you say to yourself, just a little more, just a bit more. You see, you fool yourself into doing that bit more. You do this a whole bunch of times, and each time you get a little bit more tired."

"Mr. Proffitt, I hardly see—" Amelia started, but Shiloh held up his hand to stop her.

"And after a while, you can't do it anymore," he said, almost in a whisper. "So you say, 'Lord, just a bit more, please let me go on a little more.' And every blessed time you ask, he gives you the strength or the luck. But eventually you stop asking, because you're not sure you want his help anymore."

"Is that what it is?" Amelia asked in a small voice. "You're not sure anymore?"

"Yes," Shiloh said, "Lord knows I need him. But it's different after that. And soon you're thinking that the only thing over the hill you're climbing is another hill, only steeper. Finally you find yourself saying, 'Just let the next hardcase son of a bitch I meet shoot my sorry ass to hell.'"

A small frown appeared on Amelia's face, but Shiloh could tell that she was not shocked by what he had said. The room fell quiet. "Well, you best go and see to Chris," she said. "He's probably still out there with the pigs, waiting for one of them to give him a chance with his bird gun."

Shiloh didn't know why he told Amelia what he did. Certainly, he believed it to be the truth; at least all of the truth he had words for. But to talk that way on a sunny morning and cold-sober made him nervous. Now, as he rode to town with Brady, more thoughts entered his head. He longed to be back in the kitchen with Amelia, to look into her steady blue eyes as he spoke, and to watch her head nod slightly with understanding. She was a good woman. Brady had done well for himself.

They were riding stirrup to stirrup along the well-traveled road. Shiloh had tipped his hat down low over his eyes and watched the distant western mountains with a lazily upturned head. It was pretty country, so pretty that he almost began liking it again. And then he thought that maybe it wasn't the country he had grown to dislike, but the people. The gold and silver had turned them mean, greedy, and petty.

"You haven't said more than two words since we left," Brady put in, turning a questioning eye toward Shiloh. "You wouldn't be having second thoughts about meeting that widow lady, now?"

"Not having second thoughts," Shiloh replied, "just some more of the first ones."

"You plan on telling me, don't you," Brady asked, "what it is that has you saying grace and courting?"

Shiloh considered the question before speaking. "Does it matter? People change, is all."

"It's just that I would hate like hell to say that I was there when Shiloh was brought to ground, and didn't know why."

"I told Amelia," Shiloh said hesitantly. "She'll tell you when she gets around to it."

Brady showed no surprise at this; instead, he just nodded to indicate that the question was all but settled. "She's a fine one for that. I expect you told her the truth."

"Told her I was tired of it," Shiloh offered.

They rode on in silence for a time, then the road sloped gently up, and the town appeared. Copley lay low in a wide basin. Telegraph wires stretched out south to Bodie and west to the mountains. Some of the buildings were of brick, and many were two stories. The horses, carriages, and wagons moved along a wide street that boasted a quiet prosperity. It was a town that called out, "Come here and live, but keep riding if you have a mind to get rich."

"I suppose it don't look like much," Brady said, as they turned down the road to town. "Not what you're used to anyway, after the likes of Bodie and Virginia City."

"Are the saloons in a habit of serving liquor?" Shiloh asked as they made their way down the street.

Brady's face broke easily into a wide smile. "That they are, friend." He chuckled. "Worse than some, but a damn site better than most."

6

"THIS IS IT," Brady said, climbing down from his horse and hitching it to the post in front of a saloon. "It isn't much, but it's all there is."

Shiloh studied the main street again, turning his head first one way, then the other. It looked to be a fine town. A white, low-steepled church stood at one end of the street and a courthouse at the other. Between the two of them were ten or twelve solid-looking buildings. There was pride here. Shiloh took a quick inventory, noting the general merchandise, a ladies' millinery, gunsmith, funeral parlor, and small hotel. The sheriff's office, jail, and telegraph were housed directly across the street in a wide, solid-looking structure of red brick.

"Looks just fine," Shiloh said, stepping down and hitching his horse next to Brady's. "Real friendly."

"That it is," Brady answered. Then, as if to prove the point, he exchanged howdies with two men who walked past on the boards. A wagon came by, with a rancher up on the seat, and more howdies were passed.

"Why exactly are we in town?" Shiloh asked as they stepped into the saloon.

Brady walked to the end of the bar without answering, then leaned against the polished mahogany. "A sack of flour," Brady said. "And to post some letters."

"A long ride, isn't it, for a sack of flour?" Shiloh replied, laying a coin on the bar.

Brady nodded toward the bartender, who was pouring for two other men at the opposite end of the bar. "Mostly we're here to drink whiskey," Brady answered. "Drink whiskey and get out from under Amelia's feet while she sweeps the house and maybe writes some more letters. She once sent me riding out for a thimble and blue thread. And wouldn't you know, by the time I rode back, I had forgotten both of them."

"Seems to me you're running a loose outfit," Shiloh said.

The bartender was in front of them now. Brady ordered whiskey for both and slid Shiloh's gold piece forward on the bar.

"I'm not looking to get rich," Brady said, lifting his glass. "Just older. Got a couple of boys, green but eager, who work the stock and tend to the chores. What I get for the stock, that'll just about more than pay their way."

"And everything else is Pinkerton money."

"Everything else is Pinkerton money," Brady said. "The boys are up in Bodie, seeing about buying a few head of their own. Run them with mine. Maybe folks'll start thinking I've found some ambition."

Shiloh finished off his whiskey and raised the glass to the bartender, who brought the bottle. Two more men walked in through the the batwings then. Brady turned first, then Shiloh. Even without ever stepping into the saloon before, Shiloh could tell they were strangers, just by the way their eyes darted across the room. To Shiloh, they looked to be hardcases. One big and wide, the other thin and tall. The big one had a Smith & Wesson wedged into his belt. A .44 M & H Topstrap with a bird's-head butt rested in a cut-away holster tied down to the other's leg. Both were young, not yet twenty.

Brady gave them a friendly nod as they passed, but the pair made no reply. He turned his attention back to Shiloh.

"Know what I need?" Shiloh asked finally.

"Not the slightest notion," Brady said.

"A bath and a shave," Shiloh answered. "Nice, hot bath and a barber shave wouldn't hurt my chances with that widow lady, would they?"

"Couldn't hurt," Brady said. "And might just help, unless you're planning on standing upwind from her all night."

"You thinking about loafing here?" Shiloh asked, already backing away from the bar. "If you are, then maybe I'll head over to that barber and see what he can do for me."

"I'll be here long as it takes," Brady said. "And while you're over there, have him brush out those clothes. They may be new, but they could stand it."

Shiloh tipped his hat cordially and headed out of the saloon.

Squinting into the daylight, he made his way across the street to the barber.

Soaking in a fifty-cent bath, Shiloh lost himself in thought. He had never seen the ranch, the woman, or the orchard. The idea that came into his head was of himself, riding through a pasture at dusk, seeing a light hung by a door, and knowing that it was his light and his door. And then he thought of how fine it would feel, slipping into a warm familiar bed beside a woman on a cold night.

Stepping out of the barber's, he saw the children. A half dozen of them had their noses pressed up against the glass of the saloon, peering in as if it were the window of a big-city candy store.

Hair still slick on his head, Shiloh walked fast across the street. When he reached the boards, he could hear the commotion. Breaking glass and curses greeted him as he pushed his way through the batwings and into the dark saloon. There, way in the back, cornered against a faro table, was Brady. He was jabbing out with a broken whiskey bottle, holding off two men.

Halfway across the bar, Shiloh's eyes adjusted to the light. The bartender was nowhere to be seen, probably off fetching the sheriff. Then he could see that it was the two hardcases. The tall one had a straight-edged knife, a Navaja, and was jabbing it almost playfully toward Brady's face. The fat one was chuckling, enjoying the sport. He held a gun at either side, the Smith & Wesson and Brady's Colt.

"Shit, Billy, just stick the sombitch," the fat one encouraged. "You ain't gonna make me shoot 'im are ya?"

Brady was bleeding from the mouth and nose. His chest was heaving, but those dark eyes remained calm, going from Billy with the knife, back to the other. He worked the bottle with a deadly swiftness, striking out toward the thin man's knife hand, and working the air near the bird's-head butt of the revolver stuck in the holster.

Shiloh pulled his Colt and put a shot into the floor behind the one with the knife. "That doesn't seem like a fair fight to me," he said, thumbing back the hammer so that the two men would hear the click.

"You the law?" the fat one asked, turning his head, but not dropping the guns.

"I'm not the law," Shiloh replied. "Just a man with a gun pointed at your gut."

"This ain't no concern a yours then, stranger," the thin one hissed, not turning away from Brady.

Shiloh took a step closer, moving his Colt from one to the other in a slow, lazy motion. "You all right, Brady?"

"They jumped me," Brady answered. "Pulled my gun before I had a chance."

Shiloh looked toward the fat one, whose eye was partially swollen shut and blackened. The thin one's shirt was ripped, a streak of fresh blood outlined on the dark blue material where Brady had scratched him with the bottle.

"Like I said, you just keep moving," the fat one insisted. "This ain't none of your concern." Then he brought the two guns up. He moved slow and sure, confident that two guns outmatched the one Colt pointed directly at his chest.

Shiloh took another step forward, moving through the smoke from his Colt that hung in the air. "You better choose right, friend, or whatever happens ain't gonna be pretty."

Less than three feet divided Shiloh from the fat hardcase. He had managed to put Brady out of the line of his fire. Though now the fat man blocked Shiloh's path between him and the thin knife fighter. Brady, he reasoned, could take care of himself given a fair fight.

"Ya come any closer, an ya'll see if it's pretty 'er not," the fat man said. Two small eyes, each like a bullet in a chamber, shone dully from their twin nests of fat.

Silence fell over the room then. All four men waited anxiously for the slightest signal to start shooting, stabbing, or fighting. "All you boys, just stay real still, like you are," came the new voice from the front of the bar.

Casting a quick glance to the side, Shiloh saw the outline of a man against the glare of afternoon sun that poured in through the window. When the figure took another step forward, Shiloh saw the scattergun cradled across his arm, the barrel cutting across his chest, just under the glint of the sheriff's badge.

"Chris," the sheriff said. "What kind of trouble did you go and get yourself in now?"

"Just a friendly discussion here, Sheriff," Brady said calmly, though without lowering the jagged and bloodied edge of the liquor bottle.

"I can see just how friendly it is," the sheriff answered,

moving closer. Shiloh could see him clearly now. He was a big man, young, clean-shaven, and barrel-chested, more like a magazine sketch of a lawman than an actual sheriff.

"It was two against one, Sheriff," Shiloh said. "I was just cutting the odds a bit, is all."

"Do I know you, stranger?" the lawman replied drily, moving toward Shiloh. "I don't believe I do."

Then the sheriff was between the fat man and Shiloh. It was a fool's move. The kind a man only made once. "Suppose we start by relieving you boys of this hardware," the sheriff said; the voice carried a note of false calm.

He started with the fat man's guns, grabbing first one, then the other by the barrel. He tucked both into his belt.

When he reached for Shiloh's Colt, he turned his back on the fat man. He took the Colt, shifted it neatly in his hand and released the trigger.

That's when the thin one made his move. He brought the knife slashing back, then up quickly, the blade catching the sheriff high in the neck. As the blade sliced through the sheriff's thick neck, his finger came back on the scattergun's trigger. The shotgun roared. Its double-0 shot blasted a chunk of plaster from the ceiling as Shiloh dropped to one knee.

The sheriff staggered sideways, away from the knife, toward Shiloh, as the thin one again buried the blade in the lawman's neck. A great gout of blood spurted fifteen feet across the narrow room over the barroom's mirror.

Brady leapt forward then, the jagged edge of the bottle thrusting out in a savage twist as it caught the hardcase's knife hand just above the wrist.

The shotgun fell clattering to the floor, followed by the sheriff. Both of the lawman's hands were up to his neck as a thick flow of blood pumped in a steady, gushing stream from the knife wound. Shiloh's hand was halfway to the scattergun when the big man was on him. He came lumbering over the sheriff when the toe of his boot, catching the sheriff dead in the eye, sent him sprawling forward.

The force of the big man knocked Shiloh onto his back across the floor slickened by the lawman's blood. From the corner of his eye, he caught a glimpse of Brady. The bottle was gone from his hand and he was struggling with the M & H pistol tucked into the cut-away holster tied down to the thin one's leg.

The weight of the fat man knocked the breath from Shiloh. He was on top of him in a mad-dog rage of gouging and biting. Shiloh brought both hands up and pushed hard against the fat man's chin, forcing his head back. But the big man managed to reach down and grab ahold of Shiloh's neck, fastening his thick fingers around it in a murderous stranglehold.

The big man's back and neck were arched against the two-handed pressure Shiloh applied at his jaw, yet he kept squeezing. Slowly, Shiloh lowered his arms, and when the fat man's head was just within reach, he pulled his hands away quick. The thick head dropped quickly as Shiloh forced the top of his head up against the pressure of the thick fingers. The fat man's chin thudded down like a hammer against Shiloh's skull, blacking out his vision and sending a numbing pain down his back to his legs.

But the blow had hurt the big man more. His fingers came away from Shiloh's throat as his jaw snapped shut in a loud crack of teeth.

In an instant, Shiloh was scuttling out from under the big man, his hands slipping across the bloody floor as he pushed himself over the sheriff's body. When his hand touched the barrel of the shotgun, Shiloh brought it up, his slick hands running down the worn stock toward the triggers.

Now the fat man was on him again. His thick hand grabbed ahold of Shiloh's pant leg and pulled him forward across the wet floor. The other hand caught the shotgun's barrel and yanked sideways, just as Shiloh's finger found the back trigger. The gun roared again, blowing out a small pattern at the base of the bar.

Shiloh could feel the scattergun slipping from his grasp. With each grunting pull and twist the fat man gave the twin barrels, Shiloh's finger dug painfully into the trigger guard as the blood-slick stock slid from his grasp. In another second, the big man would have the gun. Even unloaded, it was still a formidable weapon.

Shiloh rolled, letting his finger slip from the guard and his hand release the stock. Frantically, he reached back for the Sheffield bowie in the back-sheath, with the big man caught off balance by the sudden release of the gun. If Shiloh could get the knife out before the fat man got full control of the gun, he could sink the blade into that blubbery stomach.

But even as Shiloh's hand touched the bone handle of the

knife, he knew that the race was lost. The big man was already looming above him, gripping the stock and barrel of the shotgun. Feeling the knife come free from its sheath, Shiloh rolled again, pulling the blade up from his side, but the dead sheriff's body caught him midway, the lawman's lifeless arm catching his knife hand as it came up.

Then the world went black.

Shiloh felt the pain first. It was a sharp, numbing pain. And Shiloh knew that if he moved he would surely die. Then he thought that maybe he was already dead and gone to hell. For surely, heaven didn't feel like the top of your head's been blown off. When he heard the voices, he knew that he was not dead.

"Okay, boys, easy now," one voice said. "Just around the arms, like that."

There was a wheezing groan then, followed by a thudding that Shiloh felt up through the top of his skull.

"Christ Almighty, he's tryin' ta talk!" another voice shouted.

"He ain't talkin', Gil, they just do that sometimes," the first voice put in. "Now lift 'im up again."

Shiloh opened his eyes to see the face of the dead sheriff float slowly by. It was ghostly white, the eyes dulled, and the chin tucked down into his chest. The knife wound at the neck gaped open, the skin stretched so wide and deep that a man could stick two fingers in down to the second knuckle.

Blinking quickly, Shiloh felt a new rush of pain. When he opened his eyes again, he saw the sheriff's blood-soaked shirt, then gun belt, then the California trousers slide by. A pair of large hands were holding the sheriff at the knees. Shifting his eyes up, Shiloh could see that the hands belonged to a young man. The youth looked down at Shiloh with an impassive face, slightly strained by the burden of the dead lawman.

Shiloh shifted slightly, moving his leg. His foot fell off into space. He knew where he was then. He was lying flat on his back on the bar.

Brady's face floated up in front of him then. His lower lip was cut and bruised, he had another small cut just below his eye, but he looked fine. "Don't you move now," Brady said, easing Shiloh back with one hand.

Shiloh closed his eyes again, shutting out the painful light from the saloon. Then it all came back to him. The fight with the two hardcases. Raising one hand, Shiloh lightly brought his fingers up to his forehead. A knot the size of a goose egg swelled painfully out over his left eye.

Opening his eyes again, he saw Brady was still standing over him, a small thin smile creasing his cut and bruised lip. "Lie still," he said. "You want a drink?"

"Them bastards," Shiloh tried, his throat dry, "did you get them?"

"Don't worry about it, friend," Brady said.

"That fat bastard, he got away, didn't he?"

"They both did," Brady said, forcing Shiloh back down.

7

"ENOUGH DAMN BLOOD to paint a barn," the bartender said as he shook his head. "Looks like a damn slaughterhouse." He was standing at the back of the bar, surveying the damage. The floor, the wall, and even the ceiling had been doused with the lawman's blood.

"You're best off sending for wallpaper," Brady suggested. "I've seen this before, in Gold Hill. You can paint from now 'til we all forget who it came out of, and it'll come through."

"Oh, you boys sure did a job on me," the barkeep answered mournfully. But to Shiloh's eye, he didn't look to be suffering too much. The bar was crowded with loafers and gawkers, all looking to see where the sheriff got himself killed. Diversions were few and far between in Copley; Amelia's preacher-papa and the ladies had seen to that. Now that they had something half worth gaping at, they weren't about to be cheated.

According to the local wags, the sheriff had it coming for a long time. He was a nice enough fella, they said, but died as he should have, making one fool play too many. They would now say that he had nothing under his hat but hair, and Shiloh was likely to believe them.

Brady and the bartender had propped Shiloh up at a back table and set a bottle and glass in front of him. It wasn't long before he became as much of a curiosity as the blood stained wall. His head was still hurting, but the liquor took the edge off. The doctor had come by, poked and prodded at Shiloh's head, then said he was fit to walk, talk, and do anything else he might take a notion to do. Then the squat little sawbones had asked a dollar for the expert medical examination.

When Brady strode over to Shiloh's table, glass in hand, he had a smile on his face. "Seems like Copley needs itself a new sheriff," he said, sitting himself down.

"The last one didn't make out too well," Shiloh answered.

"He was just a local boy," Brady replied, pouring himself a drink. "Wasn't much of a hand at anything else, so that made him the law. Pleasant enough sort, but couldn't hit the ground with his hat on three tries."

"That why they're all staring at me?" Shiloh asked. "They all take to the idea of me being the sheriff?"

Brady smiled a little wider and downed his drink. "Maybe that's part of it," he answered. "Mostly, it's because you haven't cleaned the last sheriff's blood off your face."

Shiloh came to his feet slowly to examine himself in the bar's mirror. And true enough, the entire left side of his face was covered in dried blood. "You might've told me," he grunted.

"Myself," Brady said cheerfully, "I've been too busy getting drunk."

"You're a happy bastard," Shiloh answered drily. "Just about nothing bothers you, does it?"

"What would bother me is being laid out down the street alongside a chuckleheaded lawman," Brady said, his voice serious. "I suppose that would put me out of sorts a bit. Trying to think up something for your marker would bother me too."

Shiloh poured himself a drink and looked over at Brady. "It was one helluva fight."

"That it was," Brady answered with a smile. "Without the law stepping in we could have won."

They brought their glasses up and toasted to what might have been.

Shiloh drained his glass before speaking again. "Any idea who they were?"

"Just a couple of jaspers," Brady said. "Looking for a fight. That thin one was a little peculiar. Mighty fond of that knife."

"And they just ran?"

"Like two jackrabbits," Brady added. "I had the thin one beat and on the floor, next thing I knew the big one hit me from behind with the shotgun and they both ran off. They more than likely figured they didn't need any more company, what with a dead lawman. Probably the smartest thought they had all day."

Shiloh rose to his feet, pushing the glass and bottle away. "I'm going to go get myself another hot bath," he said. "It feels like I've been kicked by a mule."

"You do that." Brady chuckled. "Just don't be too long about it. We got to head back before supper."

Amelia was in the kitchen when they returned. It took only one look at Shiloh and Brady to turn her mood from cheerful to dark. "I imagine I'll hear soon enough what trouble you boys got into," she said, stepping closer to Brady and examining his cut lip. "But why don't you just tell me outright, so I don't have to hear it from those town ladies."

Shiloh stayed back in the doorway, listening to Brady detail the fight and the sheriff's death. Brady's voice didn't turn sheepish, as some men's will in front of their wives, but there wasn't any pride in it either.

When Brady finished talking, Amelia turned her attention to Shiloh. "Mr. Proffitt, does this happen often in your line of work?" she asked sternly.

"It happens, just sometimes," he replied. "I never went looking for it."

"Men rarely do, but it always manages to find them," she said, turning back toward her oven. "Why do you suppose that is? Makes a person wonder what sort of world it would be if women ran things."

"There'd be less fighting," Brady said, seating himself at the table. "But it'd probably be a damn sight more frilly."

"Chris, I'm serious," she answered with a laugh that told Shiloh everything was all right.

"So am I." Brady grinned playfully. "With women running things, there'd be lace curtains on saloon windows, French perfume in the bottles, and a church social every damn night."

Amelia turned then, holding a steaming pie fresh from the oven. It's top crust was done to a flaky, sweet brown. "I take it, Chris, you prefer to stay home tonight and miss the church social?"

"Damn, was that tonight?" Brady said. "You mean we rode all the way to town and back so we could ride back in."

Amelia examined the pie with a critical eye, then placed it on the table. "You both can do as you please, but I know for a fact that a certain widow lady is going to be there," she said teasingly to Shiloh.

8

THERE WERE TWO fiddlers and enough punch to drown a mule.
As church socials went, it was a beaut. A long table with pies,
fresh bread, preserves, and the trough-sized punch bowl was
set up against one wall of the small room. A line of Sunday-
school chairs and a wallful of hats were lined up against the
other. And even the ugly women weren't sitting. The middle
of the schoolroom was packed with high-stepping dancers.

Amelia's horse-trading preacher of a father stood by the door
smiling and shaking hands and calling every person who came
through "brother" and "sister." Each would linger momentarily,
their delay dependent upon how regular a churchgoer they were.
Every third or fourth person who came through received from the
preacher a neighborly wink and smiling invitation to attend Sun-
day services more regularly. Shiloh guessed that he was a man
who knew his business, the kind of preacher who would ride out
to a barn raising and work up an honest sweat between parables,
whiskey sippin', and generous portions of home cooking.

A small covey of hefty church ladies stood behind him
in an attitude of watchful ownership, as if he were a prize
steer. He was God's word on the hoof, and there could be
little doubt that they had put their brand to him. The women
nodded and smiled, their eyes sharp and wary for the drinking
of anything of intoxicating, immoral properties as well as
kissing or other over-familiar demonstrations that the music
might induce a young couple to partake in. Shiloh guessed
that the whiskey drinking was confined to the outback of the
building, judging from the steady stream of Sunday-best suits
that flowed through the open door. The kissing, he supposed,
would come later.

"A fine turnout," Brady said with some pride.

"Better than most," Amelia agreed pleasantly, then headed off to the table with the food to deposit her pies before meeting a small group of women who were trading recipes and gossip by the punch bowl.

The large bump the shotgun's butt had raised on Shiloh's head had turned a deep, yellowish blue. Brady's lip had swollen, its bruise extending nearly down to his chin. As the pair made their way over to the side of the room, Shiloh noticed nearly every head turn in a quick, furtive glance.

"Small town," Brady said, noticing the attention they were receiving. "Between your head, my lip, and the dead sheriff, they'll have something to jaw about for a month."

The fiddlers were working over a quick little tune pretty well by the time Amelia joined the two men again. She walked to them smiling from ear to ear, bringing along one of the prettiest women Shiloh had ever seen. Shiloh stared past Amelia at the woman. It's a trick, he thought. Like a magazine puzzle. The woman, taken piece by piece, wasn't beautiful. Her mouth was too wide, and those green eyes too large. And her hair, he thought, was a strange shade of reddish brown. For the life of him, he couldn't figure out how she, or nature, or the good Lord had done it. Because somehow the mouth, the eyes, and that strange hair all came together in one heart-stopping package. And all at once, the boiled shirt that Brady had lent him seemed altogether too tight.

"Mr. Proffitt," Amelia said very properly, "I'd like for you to meet Constance Reid. Constance, this is Mr. Hank Proffitt."

Shiloh nodded and tried to smile, hoping he wouldn't say anything out-of-the-ordinary dumb. He could see now that she was tall, nearly as tall as he was. Constance Reid towered over Amelia. "Pleased to meet you," Shiloh said.

And then there was silence. A great awkward silence like a stone lowered over the four of them. It was Brady who finally broke in, his eyes going from Shiloh, to Amelia, to Constance, then making the trip again.

"If you don't get this lady some punch, Shiloh, she might just take a notion to dance with somebody who will," he said.

"Would you like a cup of punch?" Shiloh asked, unable to pull his stare from those large green eyes.

"A cup of punch would be very pleasant," came the reply.

And somehow, through force of will, Shiloh managed to make his boots move toward the table where the punch bowl was located. When he returned, Brady was detailing a gentled-up version of the fight that had earned him a bruised lip and Shiloh a lump on the head.

"And you never saw these men before?" Constance asked.

"Never laid eyes on them," Brady said. "How about it, Shiloh, you ever see them on any of your dodgers?"

Shiloh handed the small white cup filled with punch to the woman before answering. "Not that I recall," he said, then sipped at the cup he had retrieved for himself.

"Did Mr. Brady just call you 'Shiloh'?" Constance asked, taking a small, birdlike sip. The way she looked, up over the edge of the cup, made her eyes grow larger. Was it, Shiloh wondered, the dark blue dress with its high neck and small greenish buttons that made her eyes shine?

"That's just what some people call me," he answered finally, feeling certain that she must think only disreputable types had such handles.

"I think that I prefer Hank, Mr. Proffitt," she said after briefly considering the matter. "And what business did you say you were in?"

Oh, Shiloh thought, here it comes. What should he say? That he was a bounty hunter? A tracker of men, one notch up from a hired gunslick? A drinker of whiskey? Consort of whores, bartenders, gamblers, and worse? A man who murderers, thieves, and gunslicks knew by name and reputation?

What could he say for himself? That he was a smoker of yellow-paper cigarettes, spender of blood stained money, and dreamer of bad dreams? He was not the hero of dime novels: His gun, his manners, and common sense failed him often enough.

If he lied and said he was a tinker, mule skinner or drag rider for a greasy-sack outfit on the Mexican border, it would not be as bad as the truth.

It was Brady who came to his rescue with a smile. "Hank here, he's in the same business as me," Brady said. "Sorta works for the Pinkertons, part-time."

"How fascinating, Mr. Proffitt," Constance Reid answered. "Are you personally acquainted with Mr. Allan Pinkerton?"

"I can't say that I am, ma'am," Shiloh replied. "But I look forward to the pleasure one day."

Brady choked on his drink at this. The shock of hearing what Shiloh said sent him into a coughing fit that nearly doubled him over. Amelia stepped quickly to his side and began pounding him on the back impatiently.

"Mr. Proffitt," Amelia said as she continued to pound her husband's back, maybe even a little harder than was necessary, "why don't you dance?"

"Ma'am?" Shiloh asked Constance, timid as a schoolboy.

"I'd be pleased and honored, Mr. Proffitt."

Brady was upright by now. He took both Shiloh's and Constance's cups as they stepped out onto the dance floor.

It had been a long time since Shiloh had danced with a woman who wasn't a hurdy-girl or outright whore. There was no difference between them, both charged for the privilege of a dance, either in fancy dollar drinks or a five-dollar night up a flight of crooked stairs or back out to a small crib. He was grateful now, as he took the woman's upraised hand, that the band had slowed down considerably.

It was awkward when he first took her hand and began to move around the small room. His feet kept dragging in a sort of schoolboy half-shuffle, but he forced them up off the floor. Soon they found the fiddlers' tune, as if they had been waiting for just that song.

Then Shiloh and the widow were moving faster and faster. The staring faces blurred and Shiloh danced the woman around the room. And she was smiling, a shy little smile, up at him. Her lips set just slightly firm as she listened to the music. Her hand was as light as a feather in his own, and he could feel her following his steps. Then he realized just how long it had been since he had danced with a woman outside of a bit joint or whorehouse.

He had forgotten what it was like. The way a woman didn't lean and hang on a man, but moved lightly at the end of his arm, up high on her toes. As they turned briskly in their steps, he could feel her dress billow out against his knees.

"Why, you are a very good dancer, Mr. Proffitt," the widow said as the dance ended in a flourish from the fiddlers. She said it with just enough hint of surprise so that Shiloh might believe it.

And Shiloh thought of how his mama had taught him to dance when he was a boy because he wanted to ask a pretty girl to a social. She moved him around the parlor, going "da-de-da-da-de-de" for music and telling him to mind his feet. It had been years since he had thought of that, and how he had mussed up the girl's new cream-colored shoes just the same.

"I said, you're a fine dancer, Mr. Proffitt," Constance Reid repeated, though he had not heard her the first time.

"Thank you, ma'am," Shiloh answered as they walked back to where Brady and Amelia were waiting.

It was then that Shiloh noticed the attention they were receiving. Nearly every person in the room was stealing quick glances in their direction. The church ladies stared openly, their eyes straying from the preacher and the door as they waited to see just what this battered stranger was about. In their eyes, Shiloh could see the demand for either a scandal or a wedding. There could be no middle ground.

"Amelia tells me that you know Christian from the war?" Constance asked.

Shiloh could do nothing but stare at her. It wasn't often a woman inquired into such matters.

"Mr. Proffitt, I asked if you made Chris's acquaintance during the war?"

Shiloh felt his throat go dry, but forced an answer. "Yes, I did."

"Mr. Brady doesn't talk of it," she answered politely. "Are you in the same habit?"

"I suppose I am," Shiloh said. "If you don't mind my asking, how does a woman manage by herself out on a ranch?"

"My husband, he hasn't been gone very long," came the answer. "I suppose everyone just naturally thought I'd move to town or back East to Pennsylvania. I just couldn't bear to leave."

"Are you ranching?"

"Mr. Blanchard leases the back section from me," she said, her voice now very businesslike. "Half the cattle are mine, but the price is tied to a percentage of *his* total shipment. He is also responsible for the care of my fences. I also have use of two of his hands five days a month. Come haying season, we split that seventy-five twenty-five. And with any luck, we should increase the total herd by forty head when foaling time comes. We have the same arrangement with the orchard, less groundfall, which I imagine is included under mineral rights and ends up in my kitchen during canning season."

Shiloh listened as she spoke. It was unusual talk for a lady, but even a blind man could see that she was getting the best of the bargain. "You think that up all by yourself, those terms?" Shiloh asked.

"Mr. Proffitt," she said, feigning modesty, "I'm just a poor widow trying to make a place for myself in this world."

Then they both laughed. She may have been a widow, but she was anything but poor; the deal she had struck with this Blanchard fella would assure her of that. She was also a woman who had kept her head about her when her husband died. In a few years, she would be able to ride back East in style.

Brady was at Shiloh's arm then. "I've had about all the punch and fiddle music I can stand for in one night," Brady said, smiling wide. "Mrs. Reid, would you mind looking after our guest? That is, if you don't fear the scandal?"

The woman hesitated for a second, thinking before answering. "Chris, I do believe a little scandal might do me some good."

"That's fine then," Brady said, nodding. "A little scandal might do this whole town some good."

And then he was gone, walking with Amelia arm in arm toward the door. They paused only long enough to pay respects to Amelia's father.

When Shiloh turned back to the widow, she was smiling up at him again, but this time her smile was different. "I am not a person of easy virtue, Mr. Proffitt."

"I don't doubt it," Shiloh answered, feeling his throat go dry at the thought of having offended this woman in some unseen way.

"Sometimes I act and speak impulsively," she continued, offering a slight nod to a rancher heading for the back door. "They say that is a woman's given and natural right. I will act impulsively now, if you will allow it. Stay the night with me. I have a warm fire and a small bottle of whiskey."

9

SHILOH WAS UP at dawn. Constance Reid had offered him a horse for the ride back to Brady's, but he declined, wanting instead to walk the two miles through the pasture.

He saw the steer when he reached Brady's southern fence. Stepping through the wire, he saw that the birds had already been at it.

It was hard luck for Brady, Shiloh thought, though knowing that even the loss of a prime piece of beef would not diminish his friend's good humor. But then, as Shiloh stepped closer, he saw the blood. A great pool of blackened blood had soaked into the ground. Shiloh felt for the Colt at his side, thinking of rustlers who might return or still be close by. More than likely they had left the steer to speed-butcher later.

Shiloh couldn't see the wound, but there was so much dried blood at the animal's neck that the wound could only have been made with a gun—a rifle, most likely. Two sets of impressions in the thick grass told part of the story. The animal had been tipped over while it slept—a schoolboy prank—then shot in the neck. The first bloodless impression in the grass was made when the steer fell; the second, as it got to its feet, only to drop and die a few feet away.

Now he saw that the animal had not been killed by rustlers. It's head had been worked over pretty good, kicked and sliced with a sharp knife, like a razor. Whoever killed the steer meant business. Water rights, a land dispute, the steer could have been killed for any reason.

Shiloh quickened his step, wanting to make Brady's house as soon as possible. When he saw the smoke rising from Brady's chimney, he felt better. Amelia would be in the kitchen cooking bacon, ham, eggs, and biscuits in the enormous oven. More than likely, Brady would still be in bed, sleeping off whatever whiskey he had managed to get outside of the social the night before.

Making his way closer, Shiloh came up on the back end of the barn. He could see the pigsty, its fence painted white. Only Christian Brady would paint a sty white, Shiloh mused.

When he reached the fence to the sty, Shiloh peered in over the top rail. Brady had seven or eight pigs, fancy breeds, like China Whites. They were, oddly enough, his favorite livestock. But now they were dead. The sight hit Shiloh like a board over the head. Every pig in the sty lay stretched out in moist dirt, each with two or more bullet holes in it. The sole survivor was a small pinkish piglet, not more than a week old, who persisted in pathetic diligence, working its way among its dead siblings to clasp the sow's cold teat.

The pigs had not been as easy to kill as the cow. But now Shiloh could see that it was the work of a large gun, .50 caliber, judging from the wounds. Shiloh guessed it was a Henry or big Remington.

Pulling his Colt from its holster, Shiloh edged his way around the barn. If Brady still had company, Shiloh wanted to see them before they saw him. As he peered carefully around the barn's corner, he pulled the hammer back.

What Shiloh, saw took his breath away. The yard was filled with death. The chickens, the goat, all the livestock were slaughtered and strewn across the dirt. The entire scene was unnaturally quiet.

Brady sat on the porch in a filthy and bloodstained nightshirt. He had one hand raised above his head against a pillar, his face a grosteque and bloodied mask.

For an instant, Shiloh was frozen in his boots, unable to move. Then, with his finger still on the Colt's trigger, he moved across the yard to Brady. Five or six lanterns and house lamps formed a jagged semicircle around the tableau; some still burned, others had been knocked over or burned out.

When Shiloh was a few feet away, he could see that Brady was not lifting his arm of his own accord. His hand was secured to the pillar with ten-penny nails that had been driven through his palm and wrist. His face was all but unrecognizable. Whoever had done it had worked him over savagely. He had been shot high in one leg, and the other was busted and twisted back at the knee. They had knocked all of his teeth out, then slit his mouth back on both sides to his ears. His nose had been broken, then slit up, under the bone, and left to hang in an obscene flap of skin.

The arm that wasn't nailed up was broken below the elbow; a shard of white bone protruded through the torn and bloodied material of his shirt. Every finger on the hand had been methodically bent back to the wrist. And they had tried to scalp him. A clump of matted, bloodied hair was pulled back halfway up his skull.

The only thing they had not touched were Brady's eyes. Shiloh supposed that they had good reason. They wanted him to see what they were doing to his wife, Amelia. Her lifeless and mutilated body lay a few feet away. They had begun with her face and worked their way down. From the looks of it, they had used a razor on her.

Shiloh couldn't bare to look at her. Turning away, he heard a noise. Whirling in his tracks, he brought the Colt up to see a fading life in Brady's eyes. As he approached, Brady made another sound, this one deep in his throat. It was a wet rasp followed by a choking cough that released a clotted bloody flow from Brady's horribly mutilated mouth.

Brady was a dead man and Shiloh knew it. But he knelt down in front of him anyway. Grabbing ahold of Brady's belt, he pulled him up so that he was partly resting against the pillar to which he was nailed. If he lived another minute, it would be a miracle.

Shiloh knew it wasn't the time to waste breath. "Was it those boys from yesterday?" Shiloh asked, looking into Brady's eyes, which grew wider.

Brady made another sound in his throat. He was trying to talk, but the words never came out.

"It was them, wasn't it?" Shiloh said, not expecting an answer, but seeing one in his friend's eyes.

Then Brady did the most exceptional thing Shiloh had ever seen. Releasing a great moaning gasp of air, he thrust his chest out against the tattered material of the bloodied nightshirt. His entire torso stiffened and lurched just slightly forward and his eyes became wild. For an instant, they weren't the eyes of a man about to die, but of one looking for vengeance.

Shiloh reached down and held Brady's head, lifting it up by the bloodied chin. He could feel bone rubbing slightly on bone, and knew that the jaw was broken as well. "Listen to me, friend," Shiloh said. "They're both dead. This is the last thing you're gonna hear. By God I swear I'll track them down for you and kill them."

Brady shut his eyes slowly and died. His last breath rattled up through his blood-filled lungs just as the sun came over the peaked roof of the house.

Shiloh stood for a long time, staring out toward the hills. The pasture, the great stretch of blue sky, the mountains, had all remained unchanged. Whatever beauty Shiloh had seen in them when he arrived, now seemed just another mocking snub of nature.

Then, turning back toward the bodies, Shiloh saw the Hudson Bay ax. Blood stained its blunted end and handle. No doubt, the murderers had used it to secure Brady to the porch, then worked him over with the blunt end.

Picking up the tool, Shiloh felt the moist blood on his hand. Then, very deliberately, he moved to the small porch and began working to free Brady. He began cutting just above the spot where Brady was nailed up. It was easy work, the dried wood coming away in large chips. When he cut through at the top, he began on the bottom. The section of pillar fell away, thumping to the boards with Brady's arm and releasing a low, groaning creak from the roof that now tilted unevenly.

Grabbing his friend under the arms, Shiloh dragged him off the porch and into the yard. He laid Brady out neatly, next to his wife, then went into the house for something to cover both of them.

Shiloh had to swallow back a new pain when he saw the inside of the house. Every stick of furniture and every piece of glass lay broken and strewn across the floor. A small fire still burned in the large oven, its doors now splattered with blood. Shiloh did not need to look for his five thousand in gold; the saddlebag that held it was hidden in the oven. Now it lay empty among the clothes and busted dishes that were scattered everywhere.

The parlor held the same horror. The murderers had spared nothing, not even Amelia's sewing basket. In the bedroom, they had overturned the bed, slit the down mattress, and emptied the dresser drawers across the floor. The room smelled of perfume and powder from the broken jars that crunched under Shiloh's boots.

Finding a quilt, Shiloh made himself walk back out through the house and cover the two bodies.

He was not surprised by what he discovered in the barn. Four dead horses lay in their stalls, their blood soaking into beds of fresh hay. Each one had been shot in the head by the same gun that killed the steer.

When he walked from the barn, blinking into sunlight, Shiloh saw the figure pulling the quilt back over the bodies. He was wearing a dark, wide-brimmed hat and black frock coat; standing uneasily next to the man was a fat swayback. Hearing Shiloh behind him, the figure turned his bulk awkwardly to stare in open-mouthed horror.

Shiloh recognized him as Amelia's father. "Now brother," the fat man stammered, "what in the good Lord's name has happened here?"

Still numb, Shiloh raised both hands. The gesture of pained ignorance revealed his bloodied palms and sent the preacher into a fit of hapless rage. When Shiloh took a step closer, the preacher went for his horse, backing away cautiously, then throwing caution to the wind as the panic hit him. Twice he missed the stirrup, then finally pulled himself up by the apple, twisting sideways in the saddle.

Shiloh moved closer as the preacher seated himself and dug his unspurred heels frantically into the animal's flanks, sending the horse in a confused circle.

"Preacher, I need to . . ." Shiloh called to the man as he took another numb step forward. But the preacher was gone, his horse finding a direction and taking up a looping gallop around the side of the house to the road.

Shiloh could not blame the preacher. The sight of the dead livestock and the quilt-covered bodies would send almost any man jackrabbiting home. Crossing the yard, past Brady and his wife, Shiloh took a seat on the bloody steps of the porch. He had no doubt that the preacher would fetch back men. No doubt at all.

"Oh, Brady, you poor dead bastard," Shiloh whispered to the covered body. "They came before daylight and you put up a fight. I'll kill those sonsabitches for you, or I'll be seeing you soon in the trying."

He talked to Brady for the better part of an hour, feeling the day grow warm and watching the shadows slowly shift across the yard. He did not address Amelia. He could find no words for the dead woman, yet he knew, that in life, she would have listened. She would have listened and thought of what was said. Then she would have spoken up when she had something to say.

10

THEY SHOWED UP a little before noon. There were at least a dozen of them, riding in two ragged columns, moving at a slow trot. The dust they raised could be seen from more than a mile off. When they were closer, Shiloh could hear the horses' hooves on dirt, the far-off rattle of bridles and the creak of leather. A dozen men or more, and not one voice broke the buzzing noon silence.

Shiloh brought his gaze up from the bodies to study the procession as they turned in from the road to the Bradys' ranch. Shopkeepers in suits, clerks in shirtsleeves, and ranch hands in work clothes, they spread out to form a single line as they rounded the corner of the house. The posse came well-armed—shotguns, hunting rifles, and pistols were leveled at Shiloh.

"You just move real slow and easy, son," the oldest of them said.

"Throw down that gun," another one put in.

Shiloh rose slowly from the steps, keeping his bloodied hands where the men could see them. "You think I did this?" he asked.

"I ain't saying you did or didn't," the older man replied reasonably as he raised his rifle a bit. "I'm just telling you to pull that gun nice and slow, then throw 'er down."

Shiloh heard a half dozen hammers click back as he lowered one hand to his holster. Then, lifting the gun out with two fingers, he extended it in front of him.

"You just lay it on down on the ground," the older one, now obviously seen as the leader, instructed. Shiloh took him for a rancher. He was lean, with a face like old leather. Everything about his manner said that he was a person in the habit of having people do as he said.

Shiloh knelt to place the pistol on the ground in front of him, then rose as he took a step back. The posse seemed visibly relieved that they had passed this point without bloodshed.

"That sticker too," the leader said, nodding, his voice low and serious.

Sliding the Sheffield bowie from his back sheath, Shiloh placed it next to the Colt.

"I found them here, this morning," Shiloh said, motioning with his head toward the quilt-covered bodies.

The leader didn't answer, but rather turned his head to the man next to him. A young lanky clerk with a pitted face stepped down from his horse. He had a short length of rope, cut for the occasion, and he used it to tie Shiloh's hands. Then he tucked the Colt into his belt and the knife into his back pocket.

Another man, farther down the line, came off his horse and walked toward the covered bodies. Shiloh noticed a moment of hesitation, then he pulled back the quilt. "Sweet, merciful Jesus," he whispered as what was left of Brady and his wife came into view. Tearing his gaze from the sight, he said, "Mr. Parker, you best come look at this."

The leader stepped down from his horse and four or five other men followed suit. They walked across the yard toward the uncovered bodies, but what they saw pulled all but the leader up short.

Parker studied the grisly remains, then lifted his head up to Shiloh. The expression on his face did not change. The thin-lipped frown and squinting coal-hard eyes seemed set in granite. It was the face of a man figuring a sum of numbers in his head.

When Parker turned his gaze from Shiloh, it was with a slight nod. "J.P., Toby," he said, looking toward the men, "have a look around." Parker then pulled the quilt back over the bodies and lifted himself from a kneeling position, his eyes turning back to Shiloh. Parker sighed deeply, then turned his back to Shiloh as he walked a few steps to confer with one of the older members of the posse in a muffled whisper.

The two remaining men came down from their horses, handed the reins over to a young clerk, who by now held a handful, and made their way to the barn.

Then, one of the men, a husky farm boy, broke his shocked gaze from the quilt-covered bodies and turned suddenly on his boot heels. His face was a mask of disgust, his eyes wide with the sight of Brady and Amelia. "Sonofabitch, bastard," he grunted and made for Shiloh.

Raising his bound hands up in front of him, Shiloh took a step back. But his retreat was halted by the two men guarding him. The farm boy hit Shiloh straight on. His big fists worked in clumsy but powerful punches, first at Shiloh's head, then at his chest and stomach. The first blow fell like a hammer across Shiloh's temple, sending a dull flash of pain through him.

The second punch caught him on the jaw, snapping his head around and sending him back against the two guards. The boy, tears welling up in his eyes, came in a third time. He took the two steps at a run, putting his full weight behind a blow that caught Shiloh high in the stomach, knocked the breath from his lungs and lifted him clean off his feet. The two of them toppled backward through the grasp of the two guards. Shiloh hit the ground hard, the fall jarring through his body and snapping his jaw shut. And instant later, the boy came down right on top.

The boy got a dozen or more good blows in before the two men pulled him off by the arms, kicking and cursing. Still gasping for air, Shiloh started to his feet.

"You just better stay down there for a spell," one of the guards, winded by the scuffle with the boy, said. "It's likely safer for all concerned."

The boy was breathing hard, but was eager to finish the job; he would have beat Shiloh to death, if one of the guards hadn't blocked the way with a shotgun. The guard kept pushing him back, using the shotgun's barrel across his chest. But the boy kept coming, dancing first to one side, then the other. Finally, he settled for spitting over the guard's shoulder at Shiloh.

The two men came from the barn, their faces flushed and excited. "Parker, everything's dead," one called. "Horses, goats, every blessed thing."

"Shot the pigs, Parker," another called from around the barn. "All dead,'cept for one little one."

Two other men emerged from the house then. Shiloh had not seen them enter. Now, they stood on the blood-soaked porch, hats off, grimly shaking their heads.

Parker broke off talking with the other man and walked over to where Shiloh sat in the dirt. "You want to tell your part of it now?" he asked, looking down at Shiloh.

Spitting into the dirt, Shiloh raised his head, "Not anything to tell," he said. "I came back this morning and found them.

Brady was nailed up to the porch. I cut him down and then the preacher came."

One of the men had fetched a rope from his horse and was standing next to Parker. Shiloh didn't need to ask what it was for.

"You came back?" Parker asked. "You mind telling me where from?"

Shiloh hesitated, his eyes falling away from Parker's.

"Where'd you come back *from* this morning?" Parker repeated, his voice going hard.

"I was paying a visit," Shiloh said, knowing that wouldn't do.

"What kind of visit were you paying?" one of the other men asked.

"Parker, we're wasting time here," the farm boy put in. "I say we just do it. You seen what this sonofabitch done to them."

"Son," Parker said, hunkering down to look Shiloh in the eye, "these boys are going to put that rope around your neck and hang you, right from that hayloft, if you don't start telling them a story."

They were all crowded around now. Shiloh sat in the dirt at the center of the loose circle of men. The one with the rope kept running his hands over it nervously.

"Mrs. Reid's place," Shiloh said at last.

"He's a lyin' dog," the boy answered quickly. "You all seen what he done to them!"

"You mean to say you were with her," Parker asked, "all night?"

"He's lyin'," the boy said again, and this time four or five of the men made sounds like they agreed.

"I came back at dawn," Shiloh said. "You can ask her."

It was three miles over road to Constance Reid's ranch. They hitched Shiloh to a horse and walked him, still bound with his hands in front. The posse, less two men who stayed behind to rig a wagon for the bodies, formed a moving circle around Shiloh. They rode in silence, keeping their guns on him the entire way.

When they finally made the ranch, it was Parker who climbed down from his horse and went up to the door. The widow answered quickly. Through the shadows and around the men that guarded him, Shiloh could see that she had been baking; a thin dusting of flour clung to the front of her apron, the green dress she wore, and her face.

For the briefest instant, her eyes locked with Shiloh's. Then she extended the door wider, and Parker stepped inside, taking his hat off as he vanished into the shadows of the house.

"You're goin' to hang for what you did to them," the farm boy said. "I got myself a mind to shoot you now, like a dog, only Mr. Parker wouldn't like it."

"I didn't kill them," Shiloh said, his voice a tired whisper. This was bad, he thought, but he was still breathing. He could not blame the men. He had made the acquaintance of some the night before and thought them decent folks. Oddly, he still thought of them as such, even if they were planning to lynch him.

But worse, to Shiloh's way of thinking, was that the two killers were putting miles behind them. Even now, if the men cut his ropes and gave him the fastest horse they could find, it would be hard work tracking the two men. He could lay blame on the strangers, but that would do little good now. The posse was not likely to believe anything he said, not so soon after seeing the bodies.

It was a killing that worked at a man's brain, demanding a justice. Shiloh felt it, and so did the men who held him prisoner.

Parker was not long in the house. He soon appeared in the door, putting his hat back on and turning slightly to say good-bye to the widow. Stone-faced, he stepped down the stairs from the front porch and approached the posse. "She says she rode you back to Brady's place last night in her buggy," Parker informed Shiloh. "I didn't see no call to say she's lyin'."

"She ain't about to take up with no drifter," one of the men said. "She's as fine a lady as they come."

"We're wasting time," another put in.

"I say we hang the sonofabitch," the farm boy hissed loudly.

This suggestion was met by a general mumbling of agreement from the posse.

Parker took off his hat and drew a large hand through his hair. "You boys reckon we should hang him from the widow's porch?" he asked.

"We got trees," the farm boy said. "And we got telegraph poles. You seen what he done to them."

"I saw it, just like you, Daniel," Parker said, putting his hat slowly back on his head. "But we also got a judge, and I reckon we can find ourselves a jury, too."

As they started back along the road, Shiloh addressed Parker. "I didn't kill them," he said.

"That ain't for me to say," Parker replied without looking down from his horse at Shiloh.

"Just the same, I'm obliged," Shiloh said.

"Well, don't be too damn obliged," came the answer. "I wouldn't bet cowshit against biscuits that you'll see next week."

11

THE POSSE ESCORTED Shiloh down Copley's main street, through the sheriff's office, and into one of the town's two cells. The dead lawman had left no deputy behind. Only a fool works for a fool, and the sheriff had been unable to find any suitably addled help. It was up to Parker and his posse to stand guard over the prisoner.

As far as Shiloh could tell, they worked in twelve-hour shifts. They did not speak to their prisoner, except to tell him that, at risk of defeat come re-election time, the town's one judge had refused the case. It would be a week, Parker said, before a circuit judge came through.

At the end of the second day, Parker returned to the jail. "You best write down that story of your's," he said, handing Shiloh a pencil and paper through the bars.

"You heard it already," Shiloh replied, taking the pencil and paper anyway. "I don't know how many times I have to tell you."

"A few more times, I expect," Parker answered wearily. "That is, if you want to keep from hanging."

"Let me ask you something, then," Shiloh said through the bars. "If I killed them, like you said, then how come you didn't find the rifle that shot the livestock? And why'd a man kill his own horse?"

Parker considered this for a moment. "Let me tell you something, mister. I don't know and I don't care. You write that down if you want. Nobody elected me sheriff, judge, or any other damned thing. I just need to get an official statement from you."

Parker turned then, away from Shiloh, toward the heavy door that led into the building's front office. The door was open and Shiloh could see a pair of worn boots leaning out comfortably across the door. The boots belonged to the guard on shift. Shiloh didn't have to see any more of the man to know that a shotgun rested across his lap.

Parker studied the boots for a second, then turned back to face Shiloh. When he spoke again, it sounded almost like an apology, but not quite. "What I am is a rancher with a wife and child, both nearly worked sick on account I'm in town looking after your hide. There's some boys around that don't feel like waiting for the judge, if you catch my meaning."

"I'm obliged then," Shiloh answered. He could picture the men, gathering in the saloons. Maybe there were only four or five of them, talking over whiskeys. Men from the posse would talk about what Brady and Amelia looked like when the quilt was pulled back. Cursing Shiloh, they would drink some more, and pretty soon it wouldn't be just four or five men, but fifteen or twenty. Then, talking wouldn't be enough, whiskey-courage would lead them out of the saloon and to the jail, carrying a rope. Parker was the only man standing in their way.

"You'd be fooling yourself thinking I would lift a finger for you," Parker whispered, crossing the room to Shiloh's cell so that his face was right up against the bars. "I couldn't give a fiddler's damn if they hung you up."

Shiloh stood his ground, looking Parker dead in the eye through the bars. "Then why bother with it? You got a man with a shotgun out there all day and all night. It would probably be real easy to get careless."

The rancher held his ground too. If indeed he thought that Shiloh was a murderer, he wasn't showing any fear. "Because it wouldn't stop with you," he said at last. "They'd hang you neat enough, then they'd trim a tree with some other poor bastard. Maybe you killed them, and maybe he killed folks too. But I'll tell you this, after two or three lynchings, it gets a whole bunch easier."

Shiloh only nodded, but continued to look Parker in the eye.

"I look down the road," Parker continued, "and I see regulators coming in for rustlers. Then, maybe they stay on, settling water disputes with a Creedmoor. You understand what I'm saying, boy?"

"I understand," Shiloh answered, wondering if that was the only reason Parker was holding him for the judge.

"I got a little boy," Parker said, letting his hands fall from the cell's bars. "He's gonna be ten in a few months. That ranch

I got is gonna be his soon enough. And by God, if I have any say in it, he's gonna live in a place where there's some law."

Parker left then, abruptly turning and walking out through the door, over the sprawled boots, and into the sunshine. Shiloh watched as he left, thinking him a good man and hoping he wouldn't find need to kill him or anybody else in town.

The unlabeled pint bottle came through the cell's high window at dusk. It appeared on the slanted brick ledge, then was slowly lowered at the end of a length of twine. When the bottle halted its downward progress, Shiloh stepped across the cell and retrieved it.

A note was tied around the bottle, held by the twine. After removing the bottle and note, Shiloh sat on the edge of the threadbare bunk to read the note: "All murderors diserve a drink of wiskey befer dieing. A friend."

Shiloh uncorked the bottle and sniffed at the contents. It was whiskey all right, but there was also the strong scent of lye and carbolic. Shiloh smiled to himself at the gesture. It was almost humorous and maybe he would have laughed outright if Brady's killers weren't putting miles behind them. Recorking the bottle he gently placed it beside the bunk.

A few minutes later, an expectant face peered up through the darkened window. When Shiloh nodded agreeably, the man's eyes squinted with unpleasant surprise then quickly fell away from the barred opening.

Shiloh was almost asleep when he heard the voices. The guard had come in an hour or two before and lowered the lamp. Now, sitting in the darkness, he heard the sound of hushed talking. He felt along the edge of the bunk for the sharpened pencil that Parker had given him. If it were a lynching party, he would use it on the first one who came into the cell. If the first one was carrying a rifle or shotgun, Shiloh mused, he might be able to make the street. After that, he would see how many were waiting for him outside.

When the door opened again, he could see three figures against the light from the office. Then one of them brought the lamp down from the wall, and he could see their faces. Shiloh eased his grip on the pencil as Constance Reid, the preacher, and the guard entered the room. Amelia's father was holding the lamp, Constance Reid was holding a long-barreled Prescott revolver. The guard was holding his hands high and studying the gun pointed at his belly.

"This ain't good, Mrs. Reid, no how," the guard said, easing into the room. "Mr. Parker sure ain't gonna like it, preacher or no."

"Jonas, whether you care to believe me or no, we're saving your life," the woman said. "Those boys aren't fooling."

Shiloh watched as the preacher grabbed the keys down from their peg and unlocked the cell. "Hurry now," he said anxiously. "They're coming."

Shiloh didn't need to be told twice. He grabbed his coat off the cot and came through the cell's door.

"Where's his gun, Jonas?" the woman asked.

"Miss Reid," he said pleadingly.

"We don't have time to fool with you, Jonas," the woman barked. "Don't make me shoot you in the leg."

"Left top drawer," the man said.

Handing her gun to the preacher, the woman went through the door to the office.

"This some sort of soul-saving missionary work I haven't heard of?" Shiloh asked, slipping into his coat.

"We're saving your hide, boy, not your soul," the preacher said, nudging the guard into the cell with the pistol. "She came to me tonight. Told me everything. We were on our way to see Parker when we saw them. It's Jobie, he's got thirty men or more over at the hotel. They're all drunk and riled up."

Constance Reid came back through the door then. She was carrying Shiloh's Colt and holster, his knife, and a battered Winchester repeater from the rack. She handed these to him, then vanished back out the door.

"They're not going to like it," Shiloh said, hurriedly strapping on the belt and tying down the holster. "There's no telling what they'll do."

"Damn right, they won't," Jonas called from the cell.

Then the woman came back through the door with the cartridges. Shiloh tore open the box and filled his pockets.

"Here's forty dollars," she said, pushing two gold pieces into Shiloh's hand. "There's a horse out back. Now go."

Shiloh thought he should say something, but no thought rose in his mind.

"Why?" he asked finally.

It was the preacher, still holding the pistol, who answered. "Because we know that you didn't murder Chris and Amelia."

"You figure this to be the Lord's work, preacher?" Shiloh said, checking the cylinder on his pistol.

"The Lord's work is fair justice," the preacher replied, pushing Shiloh toward the door.

"Then I'll be doing the Lord's work," Shiloh said.

" 'Vengeance is mine, sayeth the Lord,' " the preacher replied sadly, watching as Shiloh snapped the cylinder shut.

Shiloh looked over to the widow then. She offered only a thin smile and a nod. Her face had a fine, high color from the excitement, but her features remained set. For an instant, crazy thoughts filled Shiloh's head. He would ask her to go through the door with him. Or, he would kiss her, right in front of the preacher and guard. But in the end, he only looked away, then crossed the small room toward the door in three steps.

Shiloh was through the door and unhitching the horse when he heard the crash of glass at the front of the building.

12

SHILOH'S SPURLESS HEELS raked back across the horse's flanks before he had his boots in the stirrups. He could not risk heading back toward the town's main street. Rather, he urged the claybank into a gallop across a small field toward a darkened house, not much more than a shack. Past the house was a fenced pasture, and beyond that, open country. He would worry about the fence when he got to it.

He was less than fifty yards away when all hell broke loose at the brick jailhouse. Even a preacher and a pretty lady were no match for thirty drunks with a hanging rope. Their cursing shouts seemed right in Shiloh's ear as the horse went through the knee-high grass in long even strides. Then came the shots. Ten guns or more fired in a ragged volley that broke the cool night in a flat echo.

Shiloh did not look back. If one of the drunken men hit him or the horse, he'd have plenty of time to see who was shooting. Rather, he continued to kick and urge the horse on, even as the posse let loose another volley. Once or twice the bullets streamed by in an angry high-pitched buzzing, but most went far off their mark.

When he reached the house, he pulled the horse so violently that it nearly lost its footing on the well-packed dirt. A sleeping hound jerked awake, snarling, and the horse panicked, the rhythm of the four-beat run disolving in lip-curling, head-tossing fear. The claybank came up in a sunfishing, high roll. Shiloh dug his boots firmly into the stirrups and pulled down on the reins. The Winchester dropped from his grasp as he used both hands against the upturned head of the wild-eyed animal.

The dog was under them now, yelping with fear. And when the horse came down, its front hooves sprayed out in an awkward stumble. Shiloh pulled up on the reins now, but the animal kept going down to the left. Stepping down hard on his right side, he blew the stirrup as he pulled his left leg free.

Then, all at once, the horse was up again, regaining its footing as the dog bolted for cover under the house's narrow porch. Snorting and dazed, its legs wobbly, the animal turned its head skyward as more shots rang out behind them.

This time Shiloh did turn in the saddle. There were at least fifteen of them running across the field, pausing to fire off another volley, then run again. Behind them were four or five riders advancing at a full gallop.

Shiloh slapped the reins down across the horse's neck and kicked him forward, his right foot swinging free without a stirrup.

As he rounded the corner of the house, Shiloh could hear the posse's bullets shatter windows and slam into the unpainted wood.

In an instant, Shiloh was beyond the house and crossing a narrow lane. The barbed wire of the pasture's fence was nearly invisible against the darkened hills, but Shiloh knew it was there—dulled by the weather, but strung tight and deadly between the slanting posts. When he was within a few feet of the fence, he pulled violently to the right and turned the horse in a gallop down the small road.

He could see the end of the lane ahead, where four posts with their invisible boundary of wire and a cross-bar stood out in the moonlight. The posse's riders were on the lane now; they had passed the running men and were closing the distance at a full gallop. Shiloh kicked back violently, thinking to take the chance and try jumping the fence. The horse was already blowing hard; he had nothing to lose.

And then he saw that the four posts and cross-bar were not an unbroken line of wire fence, but a gate. Shiloh pulled in on the reins and came up alongside the gate. Someone had left the catch undone, and Shiloh said a short prayer for forgetful ranch hands and young boys everywhere. He kicked up savagely with his free foot, pushing open the wooden gate as a volley of shots came from the horsemen.

They were firing at a gallop, but their aim was good enough. Shiloh felt the hot buzz of two streaming bullets at chest level, then another pounded into the saddle, just below the cantle.

The horse came up again, sunfishing sideways as the chunk of hot, flattened lead lodged itself into the animal's flesh. Shiloh caught a glimpse of the approaching men as the horse turned. There was less than a hundred yards between them. When the horse came back down, Shiloh slapped the reins down hard and kicked his heels back savagely, cursing through clenched teeth. The frightened and wounded animal took off in a dirt-kicking gallop, its fear and pain driving it to a bone-jarring speed that lengthened the distance between Shiloh and the posse.

A small wooded hill loomed up a half mile away. Copley was now behind him, ahead lay freedom.

The horse was worked into a lather, a pained and gasping breath snorting out through its nose. Shiloh had no desire to run the beast to death, but if he made the trees, he could elude the posse.

The hill, with its thick cover of trees, was his only chance. Shiloh quit cursing the animal and urged it on with wheezing encouragement and steady backward kicks along its sweat-slicked sides. As the hill drew closer and closer, Shiloh flattened himself out along the animal so that his face was nearly touching the roached mane.

A dozen more shots sang out from the approaching horsemen, but none came close. The distance between Shiloh and the men had lengthened. Their shouts seemed a long way off. With each long-strided beat of the horse's hooves, the sure freedom of the trees came closer. And the horse, sensing that the race was nearly complete, began running with a renewed speed. The posse seemed to fall away in the distance.

Shiloh didn't see the stream until he was almost on it. A narrow brook divided the pasture from the hill. Although less than five feet across, its bank dropped off nearly that deep to its rocky bed. The stream was the pasture's natural boundary and the reason no fence was needed.

Shiloh's head burned with murderous anger as the horse almost threw him as it pulled up sharply at the stream's bank. Shiloh reined the animal to the left, already knowing that the animal was nearly spent. And that's when one of the posse's bullets found the animal.

The sound of the distant shots and gasping cry of pain from the horse sounded in Shiloh's ears almost together. The horse came down slowly under him, back end first. Turning toward the posse, he saw the gunman against the moonlight. He was sitting straight up in the saddle on his own still horse, rifle raised for another shot.

Shiloh swung his foot from the stirrup as the second shot echoed across the field. The bullet hit him high, up under his left arm, knocking him from the saddle and down the stream bank.

Another shot rang out, and the horse cried out again in confused animal pain. Looking up, Shiloh opened his eyes to the horrifying sight of the horse toppling over the small ledge onto him. A blinding flash of white pain cut through his shot arm as he rolled, kicking away from the falling horse. With the first roll he felt the icy water of the stream.

Then the horse was falling, all four hooves completely off the ground, neck twisting back toward the solid footing of the stream's bank, and its yellow-toothed mouth straining against the bit in a cry of pain. When Shiloh rolled again, one kicking hoof caught him on the leg, just above the boot top.

Half crawling, half pulling himself along by rocky handholds, Shiloh made his way several yards down the stream. The mountain water soaked through his pants, jacket and shirt, numbing him to the bone, while the sound of horses and men grew louder with each painful inch he traveled.

When they were almost to the stream bank, Shiloh forced himself to rise. Grabbing hold of roots and moist clay, he pulled up erect, then reached higher for a handhold to solid ground.

Shiloh pulled himself chest high on to dry ground as three rapid shots gouged up the moist grass near his head. He did not look back; he knew the posse was close, and his only hope was how drunk they were. If the gallop through the pasture had sobered them up at all, he was a dead man.

Rising partway to his feet, Shiloh duck-walked toward the trees, fell, and began again. The posse fired again, and half a dozen bullets kicked up dirt at his feet and whizzed by his head. Then he heard the sound of hoofbeats; they were working their way down the stream bank for a closer target.

When he was within thirty feet of the tree line, Shiloh broke into a stumbling run. Suddenly the air was filled with the sound of gunfire. Bark chipped angrily away from the trees on either side, then another bullet found his left side, knocking him down to his right. For a second he lay there, paralyzed with pain, feeling the second wound within a finger's width of the first.

Shiloh rose again, feeling his entire side numbed, his left arm hanging useless. He stood there, seeing the dark outline of trees and knowing that he was now just a shadow among shadows to the men on the opposite side of the stream. When he heard the splashing of men through the water, he began moving again in a staggering crouch. His lungs burning and unable to draw breath, Shiloh worked himself deeper into the trees.

They're hunting me just like a coon, Shiloh thought. Just like a goddamned animal. All that's missing is the barking hounds.

13

IT TOOK AN hour or more for Shiloh to reach the crest of the thinly wooded hill. He moved slowly, stumbling and falling often as he fought through the pain for every step that put distance between him and the lynch mob. With each fall, he lay exhausted and stunned on the moist rocky earth before crawling forward to pull himself erect with one hand grasping for purchase on a tree. The other arm hung as a useless weight at his side, wrapped in the bullet-torn and blood-soaked wool of his coat.

Even at the crest of the hill, Shiloh could hear the posse. They called to each other in the darkness, their voices distant and forlorn, cutting through the night air. They addressed each other by name. Strange voices from far away, calling unfamiliar names. As he rested, panting and sweat-drenched beside a pine, Shiloh began counting the names. Fifteen or more men were hunting for him. No doubt more men had been called in to join the search.

Pushing himself off the tree, Shiloh began moving again. A narrow trail cut across the downward slope. It would be smoother going to follow the trail, and for an instant this thought crossed his mind, only to be discarded. There was no reason to make the posse's work any easier. His boots catching in the narrow ruts of wagon wheels, he lurched forward across the trail and back into the trees.

With his second step off the trail, Shiloh tripped, his legs buckling under him as the slope of the hill carried him rolling down, his shot arm flopping above his head. He traveled twenty painful yards or more over loose-packed earth and rocks before coming to a stop against a large deadfall. Pulling himself up by the rotting bark, he leaned over the fallen tree, panting, his breath burning in his chest.

Then he heard a familiar voice, far off, but unmistakable. It was Parker calling to another man. When the answer came, it sounded close; less than a quarter mile away.

Slowly Shiloh began moving along the length of the fallen tree, pulling himself forward with his good hand. Halfway down, he could move no more. Exhausted, he leaned far over the tree, lifted his legs and fell on the other side. Three times he tried to rise, but could not. Each time, he fell back against the rotting wood.

As he lay down beside the tree, he felt a slight niche between tree and earth. Grinding his teeth against the pain, Shiloh removed his coat, bending his left arm awkwardly around as the garment, heavy with blood and sweat, slipped from the limb. Pulling the Sheffield from its sheath, Shiloh cut away at the shirt just below the bullet wounds. In the dim light, he could see that they were indeed so close that they almost appeared as one. Both were straight through and had somehow missed the bone. Together, the wounds formed a trench of torn flesh nearly wide enough to accommodate two fingers without touching either side.

Shiloh's side was still bleeding pretty good. There was no telling how much blood he had lost, but he knew that it was a sizeable amount. Using the Sheffield, he began cutting and tearing a long strip of material from his underclothes, finding the driest length at his belly.

He held the narrow length of sweat-stained cloth up in front of him like a prize, then wrapped it around his chest, covering the wounds, knotting it so tightly he could feel it like a saddle's cinch with each breath.

The voices were getting closer now. Shiloh pulled the Colt from his holster and edged his way under the tree. The space was so tight that it felt as if he were supporting the full weight of the deadfall on his back. He pulled leaves, dirt, and branches toward him with his good arm, covering as much of his hidey-hole as possible.

Shiloh lay on his injured side, feeling the pain, but hoping the added pressure would staunch the bleeding. He rested his head on the good arm, the cocked Colt held firmly in its hand. Then Shiloh waited. He waited for the first sonofabitch to pull away the covering of his hiding spot, so he could blow him straight to hell.

*   *   *

Sleep found Shiloh with his finger still curled around the trigger. And through the fog of a dream, he could hear them. They shouted to each other as they worked their way through a dawn the color of fresh cigarette ash. Their voices, nearly right in his ear, sounded weary after a night of fruitless searching.

In his dream, Shiloh knew what they looked like. Their uniforms gray and tattered, they would be moving like exhausted ghosts through the first light of a misting dawn.

The entire Confederate Army was searching for him. Even the dead ones had abandoned the call of heaven or fled the fires of hell to find him. The dead marched in formation with the living, spread out across the hills and pastures in a ragged line, their feet overturning every leaf, kicking every stone. They peered down every snake and gopher hole. And all the while, the butternuts called to each other across the Tennessee landscape.

Crossing the seamless line between dream and wakefulness, Shiloh opened his eyes to look out onto the dawn woods. Though he only heard the first chirping of birds, he knew that the firing would begin soon. Gunboats would shell from the river, tearing up the muddy field, and the Bloody Pond would earn its name.

Shiloh closed his eyes against the dream. He willed himself to wake into the world of living men—and the grim comforts of whatever four-bits-a-night hotel, trail-side camp, or whorehouse he had found this uneasy sleep in. But the nightmare persisted. And the dull, fevered ache in his arm was hardly like a dream at all.

It was then that he saw them. Two rebs were coming for him. They walked tiredly through the trees, their feet shuffling along. They wore no uniforms, but Shiloh could see their guns. A rifle barrel and shotgun hung low, just below their knees. They carried their weapons like weary hunters.

"He's gone if you ask me. His shadow ain't gonna catch up to him 'til next week," one said.

"Nothing to do now but call the marshal," came the reply.

Rebel tricksters, Shiloh thought. There could be no doubt that they saw him. They saw him just as clearly as if he were standing in front of their faces. But they were playing cagey, pretending they didn't have a notion of where he was.

Shiloh let his finger slip from the Colt's trigger, flexed out a small cramp, then waited.

He could see their boots now. Not military boots or brogans, but worn farmer's shoes. They were so close that Shiloh could reach out and touch them. Each mud splatter and every crack in the scarred leather was clearly visible. One of them, the reb on the left, needed to have his shoes restitched.

Then they stopped. Coming up alongside each other, the pair paused before the deadfall. Their gun barrels were pointed nearly straight down, and Shiloh could imagine the way the weapons rested easily in the crooks of their arms. One of them was digging in his pockets for something. Then there was a pause, and he heard a match strike. The smell of tobacco filled the damp morning air.

Cocksure bastards, Shiloh thought. They're going to have a smoke before killing me.

"We the last?" one asked, lifting his rifle up a bit.

"Others went in 'bout an hour ago. A cup of coffee would suit me fine just now," came the answer.

Shiloh could stand it no longer. They were talking of ordinary things, giving no mind at all to how they were about to kill him.

In a fit of rage, Shiloh squeezed off a round from the Colt, the bullet smashing into the one on the left just above the ankle.

The man fell back with a cry of pain and surprise, the gun flying from his hands. Shiloh fired again, at the other one, but missed. The pistol's blast and smoke were almost unbearable in the small hidey-hole. Shiloh pulled off another round and missed again.

The other had the shotgun pointed down, and even through his numbed ears, Shiloh could hear the levers click back. Dropping the Colt, he reached out at the greener's barrel and pulled, yanking it sideways, away from his head.

There was a strained curse, then the scattergun went off, blowing a huge chunk of rotting wood and dirt up next to Shiloh's head. The blast plunged him into near deafness as the barrel warmed in his palm.

Pulling and twisting the shotgun's barrel, Shiloh wrestled out from under the deadfall as the gun went off again. He could feel the blast, the buckshot punching into the log, as he struggled up to his knees.

Shiloh came to his feet as the full weight of the shotgun came free in his hand. He could see the familiar face of the man now as he went for the holstered Smith & Wesson at his side.

But Parker never had a chance. Grabbing the shotgun high up on the barrel, nearly at the forestock, Shiloh swung, hitting him in the arm. The Smith & Wesson, nearly out of the holster, fell to the ground, and Shiloh kicked it away.

"Easy now, boy," Parker said. "Don't make it no worse."

Shiloh didn't answer; rather, he swung the shotgun again, but Parker caught it by the butt. Now Shiloh released his grip, balled up his good fist, and caught the older man solidly on the jaw. The blow sent him sprawling backward, shotgun still in his hand.

When Parker hit the ground, his hands were already busy, searching pockets for more shells. Shiloh moved in on him fast, crossing the distance in two steps and snatching the scattergun away with one hand.

He could feel them closing in. Hundreds of reb soldiers moving silently through the woods. They worked their way carefully from tree to tree, coming into the clear only when Shiloh had his back to them. They were stalking him, waiting for the chance to fire at once. They waited and watched for some silent signal that would send his body dancing and jerking to the ground.

Not a platoon, but a regiment at least. Gray uniforms against a gray dawn. Each anxious to send a bullet tearing through his flesh. He could fairly feel each shot, like a prizefighter's punch, numbing and turning him this way and that as he ran, until a bullet finally found his skull.

Shiloh spun on his heels, unable to find even a glimpse of gray uniform. Pulling the shotgun's twin hammers back he fired, the pins clicking down on two spent shells. The Smith & Wesson glinted near Parker, and Shiloh made for it, snatching the gun up just as the older man's fingers moved toward it.

Bringing the hammer back, Shiloh studied the trees, but still saw no sign of the rebs he knew to be there. Well, at least he could hold them off; turning in his tracks he fired the pistol, then fired it again and again. He brought the hammer down until it clicked against the brass catridge. And still not a single butternut showed himself.

Then a sudden motion caught Shiloh's eye. Off to the left,

the injured man, his foot nearly blown off, was crawling to the rifle. Turning, Shiloh heard Parker say, "Don't do it, boy! Don't!"

But Shiloh was already moving. With no time to retrieve his Colt, he raised the Smith & Wesson by the barrel. As the rifle came within the man's grasp, Shiloh swung. The blow caught the injured man at the back of the head, knocking him cold.

Staggering back to the deadfall, Shiloh found the Colt. Painfully bending to retrieve it, he pulled the hammer back and raised the barrel toward the unconscious man.

"Don't make it worse on yourself," Parker called.

The lie faded in an instant and the jolting reality of it shot through Shiloh's brain like a bullet. Snapping his head around toward Parker, he looked the man in the eye even as the Colt's barrel lowered slowly to the ground. There were no reb soldiers. The war was more than ten years in the past. And in one paralyzing instant, Shiloh knew these men were not from some sweat-soaked nightmare.

"Don't do it, boy," Parker said, his voice softer, almost a whisper.

Shiloh stood frozen, unable to move. The Colt dangled loosely in his hand.

"What's wrong with you, boy?"

Thumbing the hammer down, Shiloh holstered the gun. He stared at Parker again, the horror of it eating at the inside of his skull like a yellow-toothed, long-clawed rat.

"What's wrong with you, boy?" Parker asked again, fear coming into his voice.

Shiloh didn't answer; rather, he turned and began making his way farther downhill, the injured side hurting and the left arm swinging painfully at his side.

14

PROMISES AND FEAR drove Shiloh on. He walked for the better part of a day in a lurching stumble. Again and again, he chose a tree or rock in the distance with the promise that he would rest when he reached it. But, fearing that the posse had already regrouped, the relief never lasted more than a minute or two.

He could feel his heart beating in his chest, and his feet had gone cold in his boots. Five times or more an hour, he looked to the sun, confused about his direction.

By noon, he was well away from Copley. He gorged himself on dandelion leaves, pigweed, and juniper berries. Then he hunted plantain beside a slow-flowing stream and painfully unwrapped the bandage around his chest. The wound had stopped bleeding, but he could see now that it was an ugly gaping thing. The bullets had ripped away a large chunk of flesh and muscle.

Shiloh washed the bandage in the stream, bloodying the clear water. He twisted it as dry as he could, then applied a neat row of plantain leaves over the wound before rewrapping the bandage. The plantain, he knew, would at least help ease the pain.

Shiloh followed the stream, walking along its narrow bank. When the underbrush grew impassable at the bank, he waded into the numbing cold of the shin-high water. He did not hope for a town or even a tin-pan miner's camp. He continued on only because he knew that to stop meant to die.

At nightfall he rested, ate more dandelion and juniper, then made a bed of branches. The fever had taken hold of him by then, and he began to sweat in a shaking fit of night-chills. The sweat soaked through Shiloh's shirt, pants, and coat. It ran down from his matted hair to sting his eyes and taint his mouth with its bitter, salty taste. It was not the thick, almost sweet-smelling sweat of honest labor, but a foul scent of bad dreams, fear, and sickness.

He slept then. But his sleep was more like death than rest. A half dozen times or more he woke with a terrified start to stare wide-eyed at the clear night sky, before falling back into the blackness. Each time he could feel the weight of the star-burdened sky crushing him to the earth as sleep reclaimed him.

When he awoke, the sky was blue in the east. The fitful and fevered sleep had done little to ease the sickness or fatigue. His sweat had dried stickily to his body, and the morning chill sent his teeth clacking.

Shiloh lay on his bed of fresh leaves, shivering in the pre-dawn darkness. He knew that dying would be the easiest thing. All he need do was keep still and let his strength drain from him and into the cool, fertile soil.

It was thoughts of Brady that brought Shiloh's eyes open to gaze heavenward. The morning star, bright in the eastern sky, burned with a remote icy fire. Soon the sun would be sneaking up over the treetops. Nothing had changed with the death of Brady and the woman, Amelia.

Corrupt kings slip from life in a peaceful sleep and countries mourn. Generals fall in battle and wars are lost. But a good man, like Brady, dies, and this sorry old graveyard of a world just keeps on spinning. Maybe in heaven the angels were weeping in a sweet and mournful chorus, but Brady's killers were sipping whiskey and bedding whores.

Shiloh turned himself painfully onto his belly, then pushed up with his good hand. When he was on his knees, he forced himself to rise. He knew that Brady was not the first good man to die badly.

Standing in the new dawn, on uneasy legs, he thought that although Brady's death may have been small, his vengeance would be as cold and certain as the morning star.

Shiloh continued along the creek. He could no longer walk properly. Every two or three steps sent him falling to his knees and crawling ten or fifteen or twenty yards, before rising painfully to begin the process again.

At mid-morning he saw the smoke of a small camp on the other side of the stream. Pushing himself against the pain, he stumbled into the stream, fell, and crawled one-handed to the opposite side. Raising his head above the weeds, he saw them. They were camped at the far end of a clearing. An old man was sitting in a chair and an Indian was shaving him.

Shiloh crawled up through the weeds, both knees and his good hand sinking into the mud as he worked himself toward dry land. When he was half out of the water, he looked up at the pair again. The old man, eyes closed and head leaned back, was talking, his face covered in lather. He was naked from the waist up; his flesh hung limp and wrinkled along his thin shoulders and stomach. The Indian—Shiloh could see it was a girl—was working the razor over his face in sure strokes, pausing only to clean the razor's blade on a towel that hung from the old man's shoulder.

When Shiloh's knees touched firm ground, he called out, his voice sounding strange in his own ears.

Both the old man and Indian looked up, the girl drawing blood with a startled twitch of the razor.

"Help me," Shiloh moaned, still trying to make his way toward the pair.

The old man was out of the chair and thumbing his suspenders into place. When he began walking toward Shiloh, the Indian girl came up right behind him, razor still out. She was dressed in men's striped trousers with a length of worn harness for a belt and a tattered gray dress cut off at the waist for a shirt.

"Help me," Shiloh tried again, his chest aching with the effort.

When they were almost to him, Shiloh's good arm collapsed under his weight. Then he felt a rumble, deep down, and everything he'd eaten for the last two days came up in a foul-smelling stream of yellowish green. He wretched and vomited, then wretched again, his head finally settling back down in a puddle of bile and half-chewed weeds.

Even with his eyes closed, Shiloh could tell they were standing right over him.

"Is he dead?" the Indian girl asked with more disgust than concern.

"Does it matter a whit, my dear child?" the old man replied. "Look in his pockets for coin, dear girl."

Raising his head again from the small pool of vomit, Shiloh moaned, "Help."

"Well go on, go on with you then," the old man ordered.

"He could have the fever," the girl complained.

"Very well, I'll do it myself," came the answer.

"Help," Shiloh managed again.

And then hands were on him. He could feel them going through the pockets of his coat, then searching beneath. As the old man grabbed him roughly at the shoulders, Shiloh brought his hand down to the butt of his Colt.

Then the old man was turning him, pulling him over so that Shiloh's wounded arm hit the ground with a sickening flash of pain.

"Help me," Shiloh moaned as he looked up into the faces of the old man and the girl.

"My dear sir, you can bet your very life that we will," the old man answered, not meeting Shiloh's gaze, but instead looking down the barrel of the Colt pointed directly at his gut.

They half dragged and half carried Shiloh across the clearing to their wagon. They moved him gently, ever mindful of the Colt that Shiloh kept leveled, first at one, then the other. They propped him against one of the wheels and gave him water from a battered tin cup.

Shiloh kept the Colt pointed at one or the other the entire time. Then they offered him liquor, but he refused.

They seemed to move very slowly. Shiloh couldn't say if this was from the fever or because he had a cocked gun pointed at them. "Need doctoring," Shiloh managed finally.

"Of course you do, my dear sir," the old man chirped.

"I can pay," Shiloh mumbled. "Twenty dollars to doctor me."

"Sir, you unfortunate wretch," the old man said with a broad flourish of his hand, "this is your lucky day, indeed."

15

THE INDIAN GIRL was nearly toothless, and her left eye crossed in toward her nose, which looked like it had been broken at least twice. Shiloh studied her intently as she worked at his wounds. He could see now that she wasn't all Indian; there was some Chinese mixed in there as well. For all he could tell, she might just as easily have been twenty as forty. Life, and very possibly the old man, had not been kind to her.

As she labored over the wounds, she clucked her tongue in reproach of anyone stupid enough to get shot so bad. But her hands moved with certainty and care as she cleaned the ragged flesh, then applied a generous helping of diluted ointment. The old man looked on with something very much like pride, but not quite. Shiloh supposed that maybe it was because he still had the Colt aimed at the old man's gut.

"If this hurts too much," the girl said, "just shoot the old man."

After she had tied the bandage tightly, Shiloh laid the pistol in his lap and retrieved one of the twenty-dollar gold pieces from his pocket. The old man caught the coin neatly when Shiloh tossed it to him.

"There you are, good sir," the old man said, examining the coin. "As nice a job as you could hope for. Compliments of Professor Artimus T. Jones and the lovely and many-talented Juliet Smallwater."

"Juliet?" Shiloh said, the fever still burning in his head.

"Juliet, indeed!" came the old man's enthusiastic answer. *"O! she doth teach the torches to burn bright. It seems she hangs upon the cheek of night."*

"I'll cut that throat for you one night," the girl said flatly.

But the old man seemed to pay the threat no mind. *"Like a rich jewel in an Ethiop's ear,"* he continued with conviction and a theatrical flourish. *"Beauty too rich for use, for earth too dear!"*

"Just keep at it old man, and you'll wake up dead one morning," she said, without looking up toward him. Then to Shiloh she said, "That ointment will keep the infection off it. Not enough flesh to stitch. Tomorrow I'll change the bandage and look for infection, pus. You'll lose the arm if it starts in to stinking with pus."

"O, speak again, bright angel! for thou art As glorious to this night, being o'er my head, As a winged messenger of heaven."

"You'll see heaven soon enough," the girl replied, packing the ointment, bandages, and knife into a kit bag.

Shiloh slept then. He closed his eyes to sleep with the cocked Colt in his hand and his back against a wagon wheel. Sometime during the dreamless sleep, his fever broke. He figured that he had slept for a long time, because he opened his eyes to darkness.

The girl was hunkered down over a small fire. Her back to Shiloh, she worked a long stick at a chunk of sizzling meat in the bottom of a large frying pan.

The old man sat against a tree. A yellow-bound calfskin book was open across his lap, and he was reading by the stingy light of a turned-down lantern. *"When in disgrace with fortune and men's eyes, I all alone beweep my outcast state."*

"You miserable peckerwood," the girl said without looking up. "I know thirty Indian ways to kill a man. Each'll make him wish he weren't ever born."

"And trouble deaf heaven with my bootless cries, And look upon myself and curse my fate."

The girl lifted the meat up on the stick, examined it for a moment, then placed it back in the center of the pan. "Cut that throat and pull the tongue through."

"Wishing me like to one more rich in hope," the old man read, looking only briefly at the girl. *"Featur'd like him, like him with friends possess'd."*

"Cut that withered sack of sawdust off from between your legs and sew it into that mouth a yours. I'd use a pretty cross-stitch."

This new threat caught the old man's attention; he looked up from the book, eyes going from the girl to the frying pan. "I see no reason to be crude while I recite a sonnet from the bard," he said, then continued: *"Desiring this man's art and that man's scope . . . Yet in these thoughts myself almost despising, Haply I think on thee*—a worthless half-breed trollope—*and then my state."*

"I'll take the axe to the back of your ankles," she said, glumly, again turning the browning meat. "So's you can't walk. Burn you with a hot stick then. Start in with the eyes."

"Like to the lark at break of day arising," Jones read irritably. *"From sullen earth, sings hymns at heaven's gate."*

"Or maybe I'll just slit open your belly," the girl mused with a smile, cutting the meat neatly in two with a butcher's knife. "And let hogs be at your stringy guts."

"For thy sweet love—you little toothless ungrateful bitch—*remember'd such wealth brings."*

The girl did not answer, now. Rather, she placed a chunk of meat on a tin plate and brought it to Jones.

The old man eyed the meat with a sly smile, but went back to his book. *"That then I scorn to change my state with kings,"* he concluded, and closed the volume.

Shiloh watched through slitted eyes as the pair began to eat. They ate with their hands, taking small hungry bites from the hot meat and pausing only long enough to grunt their pleasure.

Shiloh figured that it wouldn't do to have them know that he was awake yet. At least not until he found out what kind of people they were. So far, all he knew was that they were as strange as anything he'd ever seen—the old man reading from his book and the Indian girl talking about ways to kill him. He wondered if it was some kind of parlor entertainment they did for unexpected guests, or just for their own amusement.

They were almost done eating when the girl spoke. "You plan on watching us all night like that?" she said without concern as she finished her portion and began to noisily lick the beef juice from her fingers.

Shiloh opened his eyes fully to meet the girl's gaze. She was still licking her fingers, working at them, each in its turn, to taste the last of the meat. The old man, too, looked over at Shiloh. He had put a shirt on, a dirty white collarless shirt. Very gently then, as if on a linen napkin, he wiped his fingers clean of grease across the front of his shirt.

"Who are you people?" Shiloh asked at last, turning his arm slightly to judge the amount of pain. It was considerable.

Jones brought his hands together, then parted them slowly, palms up. "We are but poor actors," he replied, "offering works of the immortals to those who thirst for beauty."

Shiloh bent his head around to study the scrawl on the wagon's side: "Professor Artimus T. Jones—World Famous Actor to Royal Courts of Europe—Performer Extraordinaire—Drama—Excitement—Romance—A Delight for Young and Old," was emblazoned in white lettering on the chipped, gilt-edged portion of the wagon's bright blue side. And in much smaller lettering: "Also Performing—The Beautiful and Exotic Juliet Smallwater."

Noticing that Shiloh was reading the sign, the girl rose and walked wearily over to the wagon. From the side, she pulled out a knot, and a canvas banner unfurled above Shiloh's head. This one read, in cruder letters: "Dr. Artimus T. Jones—Makes Sick People Well—Infallible Chinese Elixir Cures Mind & Body," then under that, in crowded letters so small Shiloh could barely read in the fire's light: "Guaranteed to Cure Rheumatism, Neuralgia, Boils, Ringworm, Corns, Gout, Scalds, Sprains, Cuts, Cancers, Fever Sores, Sore Eyes, Nervous Disorders, Bruises, Chills, Impotency, Whooping Cough, Colic, Ringworm, Liver Pains, Dyspepsia, & Headaches."

"It says 'ringworm' twice," Shiloh offered.

"Quite so," Jones agreed. "But be assured, it will cure ringworm twice, thrice, or as many times as need be."

"Sign painter in Creed was blind drunk when he did it," the girl said. And then, "Don't fret over it, I used store-bought liniment on you."

"Now, sir," Jones said, rising to his feet. "Would you care to illuminate us as to your name and how you happened to come to the sorry state of affairs in which we found you."

And Shiloh did. From beginning to end. Throughout the entire story, Jones said nothing, except an occasional "ahh," or "I see, my good fellow." And the girl only watched him with those dark Indian-Chinese eyes, which betrayed not a single thought. They were the eyes of a smart poker player at a losing game.

When he was finished, Jones rubbed his hands together in front of him as if before a feast. "Sir, have you ever considered a career on the stage. I am prepared to offer you employment."

"They worked him over pretty good in Sodaville," the girl said.

"Sir," the professor continued undaunted, "I am offering you the greatest roles of the immortal bard. Hamlet, Julius Caesar, Macbeth, Richard the Third. You will, of course, as part and parcel of your duties, be required also to act as a deterrent against ruffians as well as certain unkind and unsavory critics with sidearms."

The girl gathered the two plates and frying pan together and was taking them down to the stream. "Broke three of the old bastard's ribs," she said over her shoulder. "And busted my nose, again."

"For acting?" Shiloh asked, suddenly feeling an emptiness in his stomach.

"Not the acting," she answered, kneeling down by the water. "Not that it ain't reason enough. The sheriff tried using the elixir to cure his horse's heart worms."

"It didn't cure it?" Shiloh asked, watching her drain the grease from the frying pan into the creek.

"Killed it," the girl said. "Damned animal dropped like an empty sack, right in front of his office. If those fellas you're after are in Sodaville, I don't see us heading back any time soon."

"An unfortunate quirk of nature, you wretched insult to womanhood," Jones put in with great conviction. "The animal was thin-blooded and ailing. Jesus on his best day could not cure the beast. Take the job, my good man. I assure you that it is the opportunity of a lifetime."

"You folks have any food?" Shiloh asked.

"Fetch him a feast," Jones ordered. "You worthless wench, a feast for this good man."

When she had finished cleaning the two plates and frying pan, she brought Shiloh a slice of hard sourdough, cold beans, and molasses. And indeed, it did taste like a feast to Shiloh.

"Do you accept, then?" Jones asked when Shiloh had finished. "It is an opportunity not offered to many and not likely to come round in one lifetime twice."

16

THE NEXT MORNING they ate a slow breakfast of cured ham, and then the girl changed Shiloh's bandage. She seemed mildly surprised, though not particularly pleased, that no infection had taken hold.

"You're one lucky white-eyed hombre," she said, tying the bandage tightly around his chest. "You might just get to keep that arm."

Shiloh nodded, hoping that she was right.

When they finally started out, it was well after dawn. The old man hitched up the two-horse team while the girl tended to breaking camp.

Shiloh, still too weak to be of any real help, slept in the back of the wagon. The girl laid out three blankets in the narrow walkspace, and told him to rest. It was three days south to the nearest town, which was Silver Belle, near Goldfield. The inside of the wagon was filled with bottles of the Chinese elixir. Then there were six jugs of Everclear grain alcohol, two smaller ones of tannic acid, and a rack of ingredients that included strychnine, red pepper, and unlabeled spices. They were thrown carelessly along either side of the narrow walkspace that had once held a bed and a cooking area. Shiloh was fairly certain that these were the ingredients that comprised the elixir.

Costumes for the old man's performances hung across either side of the cramped wagon. There were also fliers and hand-bills, held in neatly twine-tied bunches. Whatever sleeping and eating space the wagon originally offered had been long filled with the tools of this strange pair's trade.

With the first movement of the wagon, the pint bottles began to rattle. They would rattle for the next three days as Shiloh slept steadily, waking only to drink water, relieve himself, and eat.

His dreams were strange as the wagon bumped and rattled its way over the rutted roads. Two or three times a day, Shiloh woke in a sweat from dreams of Brady and Amelia. The terrors were all mixed together now. They invaded Shiloh's sleep in a jumble that sent him from the Tennessee battlefield to Brady's ranch. Once, as the sun beat down on the wagon and a solitary fly buzzed Shiloh's face, he dreamed that he saw Amelia running through the battle's smoke. She ran in a panicked dash through the dying men, her face and hands a bloodied mess.

Shiloh watched her from a distance. Then he began to shout, the scream fighting its way up in his throat only to emerge as little more than a whisper from his mouth. And when he woke, the sound of the scream was still tight in his throat and the Indian girl was looking down at him with vague pity. She stared at him briefly, her face floating upside down in his vision. Then she made her way lightly back up to the front of the wagon, her feet kicking through the debris.

With each day that passed, Shiloh could feel his strength coming back. The girl had doctored him good, there could be no mistaking that. But even as he regained his strength, he wondered what sort of mess he had gotten himself mixed up in. And what direction Brady's killers had taken.

Three times during the journey, Jones crept back into the wagon to try his luck at Shiloh's pockets. And three times, Shiloh drew the cocked Colt and held it to the old man's head. The third attempt came on the second day.

Jones, looking more annoyed than frightened, grudgingly withdrew his hand from Shiloh's empty coat pocket. "I could massacre you as you slept," he said. "That young she-devil up front informs me that she knows thirty Indian ways to kill a man. She has outlined them to me in all their morbid detail. They are not pleasant. Not in the least, my young friend."

"It's not her that worries me," Shiloh said, releasing the hammer and sliding the Colt back into its holster.

"Do not underestimate the persistence of age," Jones replied, suddenly jovial. "That would be a grave mistake indeed."

Shiloh reached out then, grabbed the old man by the collar, and drew him close. "Professor, I want to tell you something," Shiloh said, his voice no more than a whisper. "I'm in your and that girl's debt. But no man takes what's mine without my offering it first."

"I understand completely, my good man," Jones said, trying to pull away.

Shiloh drew him closer, feeling the old man's Adam's apple plunge and rise nervously over his knuckles. "No you don't understand, Professor. But you will. If you try it again, just one more time, I'll put a bullet in your brain and buy that girl a stage ticket back to the territories. Now, you understand?"

Shiloh released his grip on the old man's collar.

Jones rubbed his throat, then said, "Quite so."

"Quite so," Shiloh replied as the professor made his way back up to the front of the wagon.

They came to a slowing stop on the evening of the third day. Shiloh waited, hearing the creak of springs, as the girl climbed down. And then the back door lifted.

"Town's two miles off," the girl said, peering into the darkness of the wagon. "And the old man wants to talk to you."

Shiloh pulled himself out the back of the wagon, his side still hurting, but clearly healing as well.

"Now, my good sir," the professor said, coming around the side of the wagon. "We must discuss your performance tonight."

"I haven't been quite up to reading that book," Shiloh answered, feeling like a schoolboy who's neglected his homework.

"The great bard?" Jones replied. "One can never be too infirm to study the immortal words of Shakespeare. But that is of no consequence at the present."

Shiloh noticed that the girl was unfastening the leather harness strip that held her pants up. She did so without hesitation or modesty. Though as she retrieved a buckskin dress from the rear of the wagon, she offered up a look that defied Shiloh to think improper thoughts. Such thoughts, he knew, would be at the peril of death.

"What do I have to do?" Shiloh asked, feeling increasingly ill at ease.

"Do, my dear fellow?" Jones answered with gusto. "Why, play yourself of course."

"My good fellows, you see before you a wretch, cursed in life with misfortune and tragedy," Jones shouted to the small gathering in front of the saloon. "Each and every one of you may count yourselves lucky that you are not standing in this unlucky fellow's worn and battered boots."

The wagon was pulled up sideways to the boards, leaving a small alley where Shiloh sat on a stool. He wore on his head a shapeless, low-crowned, near brimless hat.

The professor had begun his shouting even as the wagon came to a stop; now that he had a good-sized crowd in front of him, he began the pitch in earnest, gesturing grandly with the lopsided stovepipe hat he wore as Juliet Smallwater stood to the side, arms across her chest.

"What's wrong with him?" a member of the crowd asked good-naturedly.

"Wrong with him, gentlemen?" the professor answered with theatrical surprise. "Wrong with him? Why, what is *not* wrong with him? Only the possible presence of ladies prevents me from listing the more lurid and patentedly shameful details of his health."

The crowd, which was made up entirely of men, moved a step closer to the wagon with its four brightly burning lanterns. Only the fact that Shiloh had made a bargain with the old man prevented him from walking away right then and there.

"Why, not a week prior, gentlemen, I found him foraging in the hills like an animal," the professor continued, his palms upraised to the crowd. "Foaming at the mouth, diseased, shot, and an affront to civilized human beings. A miserable cur that only the most charitable of men could call a man."

Shiloh gritted his teeth down on the castile soap flakes and let a trace of foam form at the corner of his mouth.

"Show him your wounds, my dear fellow," the professor said then. "And to the members of the audience, I caution, he is not completely cured. Taunt him at your own peril, my good men."

With the help of the girl, Shiloh rolled up his shirtfront. Naked beneath, he untied part of the bandage to reveal the partially healed bullet holes. A fine crust of dried blood had formed around them.

The crowd came closer, impressed by the sight.

"And the rest, my good man," the professor instructed.

Shiloh stripped off his shirt to reveal the other scars, knife wounds long healed and the pink pucker of bullet-hole scars.

"Gentlemen, before you is the profit of a lifetime of misfortune, dissipation, and corruption," the professor informed the crowd. "Of weak flesh and feeble mind. Ravaged by the demon rum, the Chinaman's pipe, the diseased embrace of soiled doves too numerous to count. Scars on his flesh are but piddling trifles compared to the scars on his mind. They run deep, my good friends. Deeper than the bullet or knife blade."

"What you selling, old-timer?" someone from the crowd shouted.

"Selling?" the professor shot back derisively. "I sell nothing!"

"Well you ain't out here for your health," another voice called.

"No, indeed, my good fellow," the professor said. "Indeed not, I am out here for your health. I have with me an elixir. For centuries a closely guarded secret of the heathen Chinese. I bring it to you now at great personal risk. Asking only a small donation, so that I may continue my good works."

"It didn't seem to help him too much," a red-bearded heckler in a battered derby called, indicating Shiloh.

"But indeed it has," the professor replied. "It has. And it will cure him fully. Watch while I demonstrate. But be warned, for those among you with weak hearts and stomachs, it may not be a pretty sight."

The professor then produced a bottle of the elixir from his coat pocket, uncorked it, and offered the foul-smelling potion to Shiloh. The professor had conveniently not told him of this part of the demonstration. Shiloh stared at the bottle with disdain. He had no intention of drinking the slop.

"Drink it, my dear man, and feel its curative powers," the professor shouted at Shiloh. Then, bending close to Shiloh's ear, he whispered, "Drink it, you damned rascal."

Against his own better judgment, Shiloh took the bottle and drank a healthy portion down. The elixir hit his throat in a gagging burn that continued straight down into his stomach. Shiloh could feel his face turning a bright red as his eyes began to water.

"There you have it, gents," the professor touted as the Indian girl moved over and held Shiloh down on the stool with both hands. "Just two days ago this boy didn't have an ounce of fight in him. Look at him now! Just look."

"He don't appear none to happy 'bout it," one of the crowd offered as Shiloh threw the girl's hands off his shoulders and began to stand. Bargain or no, he was going to walk out on the old man.

"Nonsense," the professor proclaimed. "The elixir is ambrosia. Beloved by all who feel its curative powers."

And with that, the professor turned and took Shiloh by the shoulders. The old man had more strength in him than Shiloh would have imagined, as he and the Indian girl forced Shiloh back down into the seat.

Shiloh had just opened his mouth to warn the professor off when the old man jammed the elixir bottle back into his mouth and poured in a generous helping.

Even as Shiloh made to spit it out, enough slid down his throat to give him a second jolt.

"You see, my good fellows," the professor proclaimed. "A joy to consume."

Shiloh was up again before the old man could go on. He grabbed the professor by the front of his shirt and was pinning him to the side of the wagon when the girl knocked him to the ground with a blow to his kidneys. As he struggled on hands and knees, Shiloh turned to see the girl smiling vaguely, still holding the small stool she had used to hit him.

The professor wasted no time. Straightening his shirtfront, he went on. "Not for a dollar, not ninety cents," he boasted. "But just six bits buys enough of this wonderful remedy guaranteed to put the fight back in any man. Who'll be the first to partake."

The girl was helping Shiloh up then. She eased him to his feet with one hand, the other buried deep in a pocket of the buckskin outfit. "Can you feel that gun?" she asked, smiling over Shiloh's shoulder.

He nodded that indeed he could. She pushed it out in front of her so that it poked Shiloh at the center of his back.

"Lay a hand on that old fool again and I'll put a bullet through your spine," she whispered through a slight smile as she bent over to set the stool down under him.

The girl stood behind Shiloh the entire time, smiling and watching as the old man sold ten or more bottles of his elixir.

17

THE OLD MAN had struck a deal with the livery's owner. The horses would be boarded proper, while Shiloh, the old man, and the girl slept in the stable's loft. It wasn't the kind of accommodations Shiloh was particularly fond of, but it was better than riding the wagon out of town, then returning the next night.

Shiloh, fingering the remaining twenty-dollar gold piece in his pocket, thought fondly of the two hotels he had seen in town, even as he accepted the old man's hospitality. Though, he suspected, it wasn't all generosity that prompted Jones to invite him as a guest in the stable. Once some of those men got a taste of the fabled Chinese elixir, they just might decide to come looking for the good professor. Another gun might just serve to even up any situations that may arise.

"Is that pistol of yours loaded, boy?" the professor asked as he bedded down in a pile of soft hay.

"Far as I remember," Shiloh replied, spreading out a horse blanket for himself.

The girl was bent over, moving about, where the roof slanted low. She held a lantern and was searching for something among the pair's bags. "Keep it close by," she said, removing a Navy Colt from a leather satchel, breaking it open, then closing it swiftly.

"Unsatisfied customers a problem in your line?" Shiloh asked, gathering in a clump of hay for a pillow.

"Let us just say that the occasional malcontent is not uncommon," the old man said and yawned.

The old man had not mentioned the incident during the pitch. Shiloh figured that he must not have been too vexed by it, seeing how he sold over nearly a dozen bottles of the elixir. Most of those bottles, Shiloh knew, would be drunk on a dare.

It was the girl who woke Shiloh from his dreams. She was nudging his head, just below his ear, with the toe of her boot. When he opened his eyes, she was standing over him, hands on hips.

Rubbing his eyes, Shiloh rolled to one elbow, then came up to his knees, stretching out the tightness in his knees and back. Somewhere below, a horse knickered and stamped in its stall.

"The old man's waiting," she said. "And I got to change that dressing."

Shiloh eased himself on to his back, feeling the pain in his side.

The girl moved quickly and with practiced ease as she unwrapped the bandage.

"What kind of Indian are you?" Shiloh asked, mostly just to say something.

"The kind that kept that arm from being cut off," she answered, unrolling a new bandage. The wound had not completely healed, but it was clear now. It didn't seem likely that infection would set in.

"That isn't a personal question, is it?" Shiloh tried.

"Not personal," she answered, applying a generous helping of straight liniment to the scabbed-over flesh. "Just not important anymore."

"Been with the professor long?" Shiloh asked.

"You make it a habit to ask questions first thing in the morning?" she replied, wrapping a new length of clean white material around the arm. "Or that something you started new? You weren't asking too many questions when you crawled out of that creek."

"Just like to know who I'm riding with is all," Shiloh said, examining the new dressing.

She didn't answer at first. Rather, she occupied herself with tearing a length at the end of the dressing and tying the two ends off. "I been with him for two years, maybe a little more," she said at last.

Shiloh bent his arm against the dressing; there was pain, but not enough to make it matter. "And before that?"

"You're a hard-luck fella," she said. "And it's just the worst kind of luck to tell your life to a hard-luck fella."

"That some sort of ancient Indian saying?" Shiloh answered back. "First time I heard it."

"That's one I made up all by myself," she said, watching as Shiloh slipped his shirt back on, rose, then worked his holster on. She watched him tie down with a new piece of rawhide before speaking again. "My mother was Indian. She took a liking to things from China."

"Your father?" Shiloh offered.

"His pipe and his whiskey, anyway," the girl answered quickly. "Chinaman was the only way an Indian could buy a drink of liquor."

Shiloh knew this to be true. Chinese workers often broke the law by selling or trading liquor and sometimes opium to Indians.

The girl turned her back on Shiloh now and headed for the ladder. "You could say I was a surprise to my father. But not as much as Chivington at Sand Creek was."

"You're Cheyenne," Shiloh said, remembering written details of the massacre. It was said that Colonel J. M. Chivington and his "hundred-days" regiment killed everyone, men, women, children. More than three hundred were shot down, and only seventy-five were warriors. Chivington, a preacher turned to soldiering, assigned no burial detail. He left the bodies to rot.

"I was thirteen and lucky," she said, watching as Shiloh opened the cylinder of the Colt and checked the load. "I ran when I heard the first shots."

Shiloh slipped the Colt back into the holster and forced himself to show as little emotion as the girl. "How'd you find the professor?" he asked.

"There was a missionary couple," she said. "They took me in. Taught me to Bible read, but it didn't last long. I ran away. Then there was a trader, he had me cleaning and cooking for him during the day. At night I worked in a lean-to in the back for him. Mean bastard. He's the one that knocked all my teeth out, busted my nose. Twice. Then someone cut his throat."

"That sort of thing happens," Shiloh said, making for the stairs.

"Maybe not often enough," she said. "Took maybe two hours for him to die. Blind drunk. When he finally woke up and noticed, he felt around, and his hand went right in the slit. It was that big."

"It was after that you met up with the professor?" Shiloh said, uneasily turning his back on the girl.

"That was in Creed," she said. "He liked it that I could read. He's a big one for that."

"He treats you right?" Shiloh asked, beginning to climb down the ladder. When he reached the bottom, he waited for the girl, who came swiftly down the last three steps.

"Right enough," she said flatly, straightening the cut-off dress-top she wore over the California trousers. "Now, you tell me, you ever in the army, or you just wear that blue coat for show?"

"I fought," Shiloh replied, standing his ground at the bottom of the stairs. "Not Indians."

"In the war, huh?" she asked, smiling for the first time. "White-eye killing white-eye, I would pay cash money to see that."

The old man was waiting for Shiloh in the nearest saloon. It wasn't much, maybe even the worst one in town. The girl took a seat outside on a rough-hewn bench. She nodded Shiloh through the batwings and put on her face an expression of such open hostility that it defied any but the most foolhardy even to give her a howdy.

The professor, however, was in fine spirits, smiling around the rosiest cheeks and reddest nose good liquor could buy. It was not yet noon, and he was already on the outside of a good measure of whiskey.

The old man turned from the bar to greet Shiloh with widely opened arms. "My good fellow," he said with a laugh, "I want you to meet a true scholar and gentleman. Mr. Terrance McHurdy, proprietor of this fine establishment. Mixologist and patron of the arts."

The bartender's clean-shaven, hangdog face turned a bit more morose with the professor's introduction. He nodded slightly, waiting to see what new embarrassment now faced him. He was a man who didn't suffer fools gladly, but rather, as an occupational hazard.

Shiloh bellied up to the bar and ordered a breakfast whiskey, which the bartender brought slowly. He waited then for Shiloh to pay. The old man's good humor, it seemed, did not extend to charity.

The professor watched Shiloh sip at the whiskey before

speaking. "Mr. McHurdy here has been wise enough to accept my offer to bring a generous measure of culture to this dusty outpost thirsting for entertainment."

The bartender gave the old man a long hard look, then turned his attention to Shiloh. "He tells me you folks got a show, that true? Or is it snake-oil talk?"

Shiloh finished off the liquor in a gulp. "I suppose it's true enough."

The bar-dog leaned far over the wood then. "You *suppose* it's true?" he asked. "He tells me that you got a show with sword fighting in her."

Shiloh held up his glass for another drink. "If he says so, then we do."

The bartender had no intention of pouring any more liquor, at least not until this sword fighting question was answered.

Now, it was the professor who spoke up. "If it is clash and clang of cutlass and foil you desire, then that is what you shall have, my good man. A sword fight to thrill the hearts of all that witness it. And words from the immortal bard to thrill their souls."

The bartender turned then, reached the bottle of liquor back from the shelf, and poured Shiloh's drink. "There's two other saloons down the street," he said, unburdening himself. "One just got two pretty waiter gals, and the other has three faro tables and a French roulette wheel. They, both of them, got me beat from soda to hoc. You bring me in drinking men with a sword fight, and I'll pay."

The professor spent the better part of the day in the saloon. He sat at a back table, writing in a careful hand, across a piece of general store wrapping paper, what Shiloh would have to say that night. The girl was out walking the boards, distributing leaflets for patent medicine on one side and that night's show on the other.

Shiloh sat at the table with Jones, drinking away the last of his twenty dollars and watching the professor write. When he was down to ten dollars, he knew that he would have to head off after Brady's killers tomorrow. If he had to walk, sell his gun, or steal, he could wait no longer.

"Oh, my dear boy," the professor said, lifting his eyes from the task. "I have selected your lines with care. With a great deal of care."

"You don't need to look in the book for them?" Shiloh asked, noticing that the old man had opened the book only rarely.

"Indeed not," came the response. "The words are etched on my brain."

Shiloh lifted one end of the paper and began to read out loud, *"O coward conscience, how dost thou afflict me! The lights burn blue. It is now dead midnight. Cold fearful drops stand on my trembling flesh. What do I fear? myself? there's none else by."*

Jones was smiling a crafty old smile. "Read on, my dear boy," he said happily.

Shiloh skipped to another part of the page and read: *"Dream on, dream on, of bloody deeds and death; Fainting despair; despairing, yield thy breath!"*

"Richard the Third, my boy," the old man cackled happily. "A privilege and an honor to play, one of the bard's greatest."

"Any particular reason you chose these ones?" Shiloh asked, the words burning in his head. *Dream on, dream on, of bloody deeds.* The old bastard.

"Keep on with it, read!" the old man nearly shouted with glee. "Read! It cuts to the bone."

And Shiloh did. *"I shall despair. There is no creature loves me; And if I die, no soul will pity me: Nay, wherefore should they, since that I myself find in myself no pity to myself?"*

Shiloh let the length of paper fall to the table, the gray penciled words still staring up at him. "You remember something else from that book, Professor," he said.

The professor took up the paper, smoothed it lovingly across the table and began reading in a low, sonorous voice, *"Let not our babbling dreams afright our souls; Conscience is but a word that cowards use, Devis'd at first to keep the strong in awe; Our strong arms be our conscience, swords our law."*

"Recite all you want," Shiloh said, rising from his chair. "But you find something else for me to play act."

"You, my dear fellow, are in no position," the professor said with a voice suddenly gone nasty, "none at all, to decide tonight's performance."

"I'll walk out on you," Shiloh said, standing to leave. "You and Juliet can do it alone or piss up a rope for all I care."

"No position to do that, either, my belligerent friend," the old man hissed as he brought a folded dodger from his pocket and tossed it across the table.

Shiloh sat back down and read it. The poster looked like hundreds he'd seen before, except this one had his name on it. The Pinkerton Agency was offering a five-hundred-dollar reward for his capture.

"Who's seen this?" Shiloh asked, folding the dodger back up.

"No one," the old man replied. "Dear and resourceful Juliet took the liberty of retrieving it from the mail bag this morning."

"She just happen to find the mail sack lying around the Fargo office?"

"The poor, misguided savage," the professor said, feigning remorse. "The mails hold a certain profitable fascination for her. A habit I have taken great pains, unsuccessfully, to break her of."

Shiloh read the poster again. There was no question that he had to find Brady's killers. It was either that or spend the rest of his days running from the law. "I told you the story," Shiloh tried. "That first day."

"Yes, indeed you did, my good fellow," the professor conceded. "Though the illustrious Mr. Allan Pinkerton now tells us a more interesting, if not more profitable, tale. But it is of small consequence. A murderer of conscience or no, I shall find something more to your liking and perhaps temperament. Hamlet, I should think."

Looking the professor in the eye, Shiloh said, "You could collect this reward, or are you just making so much money from the elixir, you figure the five hundred isn't worth the time?"

"Oh indeed," the old man said. "Juliet was quite enthusiastic at the prospect, but I disuaded her. For the time being. I confess, I've taken a liking to you. You, my dear boy, are tragedy, writ in flesh and blood. Tonight, when we see what manner of actor you are, that shall decide."

Shiloh stared at the old man, knowing that he was either a fool or mad. Whichever way it was, it didn't seem to make much difference.

"Oh God! I could be bounded in a nut-shell, and count myself a king of infinite space, were it not that I have bad dreams," the old man recited as Shiloh made for the door. "Hamlet! Now there's a role befitting your true nature, my dear friend."

18

IT WAS A marvel to behold. The old man stood out front on a whiskey crate, yelling and waving his arms about like a hell-fire, circuit-riding preacher. Juliet Smallwater, sword buckled at her waist, worked stragglers in like a champion cutting horse, herding drinkers and loafers, toward the saloon. It was not yet sunset, and already they had the barroom half full.

Shiloh watched from a standing position at the bar. Soon, he was elbow to elbow with drinkers as the barroom filled with smoke. Then, at some unspoken signal, the professor and girl came through the batwings.

"Well, my good lad," the professor said, taking Shiloh by the arm. "It is time we repair to the dressing room."

Taking his whiskey glass with him, Shiloh followed the professor into a storage room filled with empty crates, new kegs, and busted chairs.

"Do you have your lines, lad?" he asked, handing Shiloh a badly bent Starr cavalry saber.

Tying the saber on above his coat and holster, Shiloh reached into his back pocket and produced the folded wrapping paper.

"Now then, that's a fine fellow," the professor said and chuckled, tying his own, noticeably less worn cutlery around his waist. "Juliet, my darling, the lights."

But the girl didn't have to be told, she was already moving out through the door to light the semicircle of six lanterns arranged at the back of the bar. Then she was speaking, performing. She spoke in a flat, nearly contemptuous voice that silenced the laughing and shouts from the bar. Shiloh suspected that the sword at her side may have had a part in her ability to silence the room.

The professor stood nervously by the door. He was in shirt-sleeves, wearing a threadbare broadcloth vest and a tin crown that had been fashioned from a can of coal oil. And he was muttering to himself. When he turned to Shiloh, he seemed a little taller, and there was a strange light in his eye. "Are you ready, lad?"

Shiloh shrugged, unfolding the bit of paper he would read.

"Good then," came the answer. "Zounds! You need the hat!" A frantic search produced a strange felt hat. It was like a woman's hat, only badly battered. A large ostrich feather hung limply on one side.

"You want me to wear a hat, then you get me a John B.," Shiloh said, not taking the proffered chapeau.

"There is no time," the professor argued. "None whatsoever. Take it and wear it or I shall be forced to—"

Shiloh cut the old man off in mid-sentence by taking the hat and placing it far back on his head.

"Good then," the professor chirped. "Let us entertain and enlighten these rascals."

And with that, the old man was through the door. Shiloh followed, walking with his head bent slightly down. Before he knew it, he was behind the lights, and the girl was standing in back of him.

The old man began then. *"My hour is almost come, When I to sulphurous and tormenting flames must render myself up,"* the old man recited with a doleful passion.

"Alas, poor ghost," Shiloh read in a reluctant whisper.

"Speak up pardner," someone shouted from the audience. "Can't hardly hear nothin' of it."

And then the girl spoke, not loud, just loud enough for Shiloh to hear over the old man's voice. "You read that paper a little louder next time," she said. "I got my finger on a trigger and five hundred reasons to pull it."

"Speak, I am bound to hear," Shiloh read with renewed enthusiasm.

"So art thou to revenge, when thou shalt hear?" the old man asked, his face not two inches from Shiloh's.

Shiloh looked down at the paper for what he was to say next, *"What?"*

And then the old man was going on, waving his arms and moving about the stage, hunkering down right in the uneven lights of the lanterns, then rising up and waving his arms.

When it came time for Shiloh to read again, he could feel the girl at his back. *"Murder!"*

"Murder most foul, as in the best it is; But this most foul, strange, and unnatural," the old man replied, nearly yelling.

"Haste me to know't, that I, with wings as swift as meditation or the thoughts of love, may sweep to my revenge," Shiloh said. And he was surprised that none of the audience laughed. Indeed, twenty-five or more men were sitting in front of him, waiting for what he had to read.

Lifting his head, Shiloh looked out past the lanterns as the old man went on again.

It was then that Shiloh saw them. At the bar, away from the lanterns, were Brady's killers! Suddenly there was a pounding in his head, his stomach turned to stone. The entire room had fallen silent.

"Read your damned bit," the girl hissed, moving up close behind him.

"Murdering sonsabitches!" Shiloh screamed as he charged over and through the neat row of lanterns toward the bar.

For an instant, none of the seated men closest to the lanterns moved, thinking it was part of the play, maybe even the best part. Then, as he hustled through the tables, Shiloh went for his Colt. There was a rush toward the stage and the door, as the crowd parted in front of him.

He was halfway to the bar before the two men turned. They stood frozen, hands still lifting whiskey glasses.

"You're both of you going to die," Shiloh spat out between clenched teeth, wrestling with the pistol. But the Colt's handle would not come free from under the belt that held the sword.

"Crazy bastard," the fat one said, backing slowly off. Then, recognition flashed across his eyes, and he went for the gun tucked into his belt.

A hot bolt of pain surged up Shiloh's wounded side as he released his grip on the Colt and drew the sword. Before the gunman could raise the pistol, Shiloh slashed out with the saber.

The tarnished blade caught the pistol at mid-barrel, knocking it downward as the gun blasted a hole in the floor. Shiloh felt the shot ring up the blade as he pulled back and slashed sideways, hitting the gunman at the hip. If the saber had been sharpened, it likely could have cut him in two, but someone had ground the blade down to a dull edge for play acting.

Shiloh drew the sword back then, to run the fat one through as he staggered against the bar bent sideways. Then he saw the thin one drawing down. Shiloh turned quickly and slashed out again, knocking the thin one's hat off, opening a gaping and bloody gash just above his left eye.

The odds were bad, and Shiloh knew it. Fighting two gunmen with a dull sword was no proper way to die. But if he was going to hell, at least he could take one of the bastards with him. Dropping the saber, Shiloh again went for his Colt. The pistol cleared leather smoothly this time.

As the fat gunman made to bring his gun up, Shiloh pressed the Colt's barrel into the soft folds of the killer's belly and fired. The big man cried out in pain as the .44 slug tore through blubbery flesh and neatly severed his backbone.

But the Smith & Wesson kept rising up on Shiloh's left side, even as the killer's legs set in to trembling.

Shiloh jabbed the Colt forward, like a dagger. The barrel pushed smoothly through the oozing bullet hole into the fat man's stomach. He could feel the weight of the big man and see the shaking gun hand struggling for a shot. Two shots boomed out from the killer's gun, and Shiloh's ears rang with the blasts.

And still the Smith & Wesson kept rising as Shiloh twisted the Colt's barrel upward and triggered off two more rounds.

The bullets ripped through the big man's guts and exploded out from between his shoulder blades. It was only then that Shiloh felt the cool metal of the Smith & Wesson at his neck, just below the ear. It lingered there for an instant, then fell away as the killer's legs gave out from under him.

Shiloh turned before the fat man's head hit the brass rail. He brought the bloody Colt up fast, to draw down on the thin one. The other gunman was less than three feet away, still stunned from the saber blow, his face a mask of blood and fear. He was wiping the blood from his eyes when he caught the briefest glimpse of Shiloh's Colt, but that was enough.

Before Shiloh could pull the trigger, the thin one fired. The bullet burned across Shiloh's ear as the world went black in a flash of powder.

Through the ringing of the gunshot, someone screamed and then Shiloh fired. Still blinded, he heard only the crash of glass. As he staggered forward, Shiloh fired again, emptying the Colt at where the gunman should have been.

Just as Shiloh's gun clicked down on a spent shell, the world came back into focus through burning eyes. No body was lying on the floor before him; rather, there was only the shattered front window of the saloon, and a thin trail of blood to the batwings.

Shiloh fumbled with the cylinder as he made for the door. He had dropped three cartridges and loaded two by the time he reached the batwings and came face to face with the law.

"What's your damn hurry, gent?" the rail-thin sheriff said, bringing his rifle's barrel so sharply up under Shiloh's jaw that it snapped his teeth shut.

The sheriff took Shiloh's gun, clicked the cylinder shut, and backed him into the saloon. When the lawman indicated for him to turn, Shiloh felt the cool steel of the barrel slip from under his jaw, then he saw the professor. The row of lanterns that bordered the makeshift stage illuminated the scene in all its horrific detail.

The old man had been hit in the chest. His tin crown lay a few feet away, knocked off as he fell. Juliet Smallwater had his head in her lap. From somewhere she had gotten a beer and whiskey-soaked bar rag and was pushing it one-handed against a sucking chest wound. With her other hand, she brushed the old man's graying hair out of his eyes.

The professor looked very old now. His face was bathed in sweat, and his mouth hung limp and half opened. The teeth, lips, and tongue were a horror from the blood that had foamed up from where the bullet had done its work on his insides. His hand lay on the hilt of the sword.

"You folks gonna tell me what went on here?" the sheriff asked, his eyes going from the professor to the dead gunman at the bar.

"The old man's been shot bad," the girl said.

"They went to fetch the doc," the lawman offered as he bent to the dead gunman.

"Doc won't help him," the girl answered, looking down at the bar rag, now heavy with blood.

The sheriff turned the gunman over one-handed, rifle still leveled at Shiloh.

"Doc can't help this one, either," the sheriff said as he rose up again.

"My final performance, I fear," the professor offered suddenly in a gasping whisper.

"Lay still, old man. Don't talk none," the girl replied.

"Dear Juliet," the professor moaned. "It hardly matters now."

"Lay still," she said impatiently, "and maybe you'll live."

A large pool of blood was leaking out from under the old man. The bullet had gone clean through.

"Dear sweet Juliet," he said, coughing, his voice nearly as small and muffled as the wet hiss of the wound. *"There's language in her eye, her cheek, her lip, Nay, her foot speaks; her wanton spirits look out at every joint and motive of her body."*

And then the old man was dead.

Shiloh and the sheriff watched as she held the old man for a moment longer. When she had satisfied herself that he was dead, the girl threw the bar rag down and closed his eyes with bloodied fingers that left small red smudges across the lids.

19

"IT WAS HIM that started it," the saloon keeper, McHurdy, shouted. "He came high-balling across in a ladies hat and swinging a sword."

The sheriff seemed to consider this for a moment, his sharp-eyed gaze going from Shiloh to McHurdy and then to Juliet Smallwater. The saloon was starting to fill up again. Word of the fight had spread quickly through town, and gawkers were lining up at the bar.

"Nothing to do but take the whole lot of them over to the jail, Mickey," he said at last to the bar-dog.

The doctor arrived then. He was young, thin, and clearly in ill spirits. Roused out of bed, he pronounced both men dead without taking his hat off or opening a medical bag. Walking from one to the other, he kicked both in the ribs and announced his learned opinion. "They're deader than hell; give me a whiskey," the doctor said, setting his medical bag down on the bar.

A general murmur of agreement rose from the gawkers. To a man, their own prognosis had matched that of the good doctor's. Only now, it was official.

"You figure that having a whiskey is gonna help any?" the sheriff asked. "How long you go to that eastern school to learn that?"

"I can't speak for them, Sheriff," the doctor said as he removed his hat. "But it sure as shit will improve my spirits."

McHurdy went back behind the bar and poured the doctor his drink. This triggered a general run toward the bar among the gawkers, who bellied up to the mahogany from one end to the other, leaving just enough room around the dead gunman.

Gawking at dead men was thirsty work, Shiloh thought grimly.

Juliet Smallwater still held the old man's head in her lap. She was still talking to him in a low voice, ignoring the quick glances from the drinkers.

"Nothing to do for it but take the both of them over to the office," the lawman said, picking up Shiloh's bloody Colt from off the bar and tucking it into his belt. "Mickey, you and a couple of these good citizens here haul the bodies over behind the general merchandise."

"I can't be leaving now," the bar-dog complained. "I'm pouring whiskey and taking money for the first time in a dog's life."

The sheriff, rifle still leveled on Shiloh, frowned deeply at the answer. "What are you planning on, Mickey?" he asked. "Leaving them where they died, sort of an attraction?"

"It wasn't me that killed them," the bar-dog shot back bitterly as he poured another drink.

"I need four men to carry these boys over to the general merchandise," the lawman announced.

The entire line of drinkers hunched closer into their drinks.

"It's up to you and that Indian gal then," the sheriff informed Shiloh. Then to McHurdy he said, "And while I'm in a mind to ask, you want to tell me what an Indian is doing in this establishment?"

"She didn't drink nothin'," came the cautious reply. "She's an actress, the old man said."

"What are you, Paiute, missy?"

"I wouldn't spit on a Paiute," the girl replied, easing the old man's head gently to the floor.

"Whatever you are, we'll sort it out at the jail," the sheriff said, then made a slight motion of the rifle to indicate that they should start on the body by the bar.

"You didn't happen to see what direction the other one took, Sheriff?" Shiloh asked as he walked over to the body.

"I wouldn't be worrying about him," the sheriff replied curtly.

Shiloh grabbed the fat killer under the arms and the girl took him by the feet. As they eased the body up off the floor, his head came back so that the two dead eyes stared up directly at Shiloh.

Even under the sheriff's gun and the weight of the body, Shiloh felt a certain grim satisfaction. Somewhere, if it were possible, Brady was smiling his lopsided grin. Amelia, maybe, wouldn't be smiling.

"Here, take your hat, you happy bastard," the sheriff said, tossing the feathered cap on the dead man's stomach.

"Quit grinning like a damned idiot," the girl hissed as they struggled with the body out through the batwings. "Don't you know the law don't like it when a murderer smiles. Makes them nervous."

"That's a plain truth," the lawman said, close to Shiloh's ear. "But we'll see how much you smile with a rope around your neck."

"That was a fair fight, Sheriff," Shiloh replied.

"Hell yes, son, I believe you," came the answer. "You took on the both of them with a sword, a gun, and a ladies hat."

They were passing down an alley next to the general store. The gash in the dead man's head had made a mess of Shiloh's pant legs and boots. And he could feel the newly healed skin of his wound tearing open. The pain burned right down to his fingers, leaving them numb.

When they reached the back of the store, the girl dropped the dead man's boots. The sudden movement caused the upper half to yank out of Shiloh's hands. The corpse hit the ground with a dull thud and a wheezing release of air from his lungs.

"Go on and pick him up, not much farther," the sheriff said.

"Stupid, white-eyed bastard," the girl said, kneeling back down. "Shooting the fattest man in the bar."

This seemed to tickle the sheriff some, and he let go with a small laugh. But he wasn't laughing when he looked back at the girl. She was holding a small hideaway on him. She held it at waist level and as steady as any gun Shiloh had ever seen pointed at a man.

"Give over that rifle, Sheriff," she said. "Pistol too."

"I'll shoot him," the lawman replied, reminding her that the rifle was pointed dead center at Shiloh's back.

"Shoot him," the girl said flatly. "He ain't nothing to me. He dies, then you die. Just the same, I ride off."

"I ain't fooling with you, missy," the lawman said, his voice hard.

The girl cocked the hammer back on the small pistol to show that she wasn't fooling either.

Then a wagon passed by on the street, and the sheriff made to turn his head.

"Don't," the girl ordered.

And then the sheriff handed Shiloh both the rifle and Colt.

"Give it here," the girl ordered. "And pick him up again."

Shiloh handed over the rifle, then reached down and grabbed the dead man.

"You too, Sheriff," the girl said. "Must be a law about leaving dead men in alleys. I don't look to break no laws."

Together, Shiloh and the sheriff carried the dead man to the back of the general store. When they had deposited him on the small porch, the girl ordered Shiloh to tie up the sheriff with the dead man's belt.

"Now his mouth," the girl said, handing Shiloh the rope that had held the sword to her side.

"Which direction?" Shiloh asked.

"Who? That other one?" the sheriff asked.

"The thin one. Which way did he ride?"

"I don't know, south," the sheriff muttered, his eyes fixed on the rifle the girl held on him. "I saw him light out from my office."

The girl cocked the rifle's hammer back. "Maybe you want to draw a map for the law," the girl said to Shiloh. "So he doesn't worry about us none."

"You folks'll get a fair trial," the sheriff tried. "As for you, missy, nobody said you did a blessed thing."

The girl moved across to the sheriff, the barrel of the rifle close to his head. "That right, Sheriff?" she spat. "What kind of trial does an Indian and an idiot white man get in this town?"

"Fair," came the quick answer. "Sober judge and a good lawyer, if you want him."

"I got a better thought," the girl said, tightening her finger around the trigger.

"Don't shoot him," Shiloh said. "You do it, I'll kill you at the first chance."

"You're worse than a fool," the girl spat back, handing the rifle to Shiloh. "You don't care about nothing, not even your own hide. And it's the worst kind of bad luck to ride with a man who don't care." And then she was gone, slipping off behind the buildings toward the livery and the medicine wagon.

The sheriff and Shiloh watched as the shadows swallowed the girl in a second. "I'm obliged," the sheriff said.

"Give me as long as you can then," Shiloh said, tying the lawman's mouth shut. "That one and the other killed a good man and his wife."

Shiloh didn't wait for the sheriff's muffled answer. He was already trotting toward the livery through the darkened yards.

He heard the pounding when he reached the stable's back door. Shiloh stepped into the dim lantern light of the stable and found the owner in the small closet where the girl had locked him before taking his own personal horse and a silver-trimmed Mexican saddle. He was madder than a nest of hornets, and his mood didn't improve when he looked down the rifle barrel.

"I haven't got no time to bargain," Shiloh said. "Which horse for the wagon and team?"

"That damned Indian bitch told me she was trading the wagon for the horse," came the angered answer. "Didn't have no damned choice in the matter, neither."

"That rig alone's worth two horses," Shiloh answered, keeping an eye on both doors. "You don't want to pick, I will."

"Third stall," the owner said. "Over on the right."

Then Shiloh locked him back in the closet.

20

SHILOH RODE THROUGH the night and into the next day. But it didn't take that long for him to know that the livery owner had gotten the better part of the bargain. The horse he rode was a buckskin-colored gelding with an undershot jaw, a rubber neck, and a goose rump. The animal wasn't particularly onery. It was just that in his twelve or fifteen years he had seen better days, but not many. Mostly, Shiloh suspected, the beast was plain tired of the whole game. He was gelded early, and things probably had not improved much for him after that.

Shiloh headed southeast toward the desert and through open country. Piñon pine and juniper gave way to sage and shadescale. It all looked familiar; another few miles to the east and he would be riding the same trail that had led him to Brady.

By mid-morning, the sun was hot and reminding Shiloh that he no longer had a hat. Tying a bandana to his head would keep the sun off, well enough, until he could bargain for a hat with the six dollars he had in his pocket. He would need a new firearm as well. The sheriff's rifle, now riding high on the saddle secured by a length of rope, was a Remington-Whitmore, a combination, double-barreled weapon with shotgun on the left and rifle on the right. It was a lawman's gun and would do Shiloh little good. He would trade it for a repeater the first chance he got.

As he rode blindly south, Shiloh thought of the killer. He had only an hour or so lead on Shiloh, but that was enough. A man could lose himself from the world in an hour. All Shiloh knew was that the killer would want to put distance behind him. He was a hunted man now, and hunted men ran. Some ran faster and smarter than others, but they all ran.

Soon Shiloh was faced with a new fear, that the killer would abandon the horse at the first depot, then begin his running on the train. In three days, he could be in Utah or Arizona. In a week he could step off the train in Texas or Colorado.

Shiloh reined the tired mare to the east and headed for the next town. There the killer would be able to find a doctor for his head and a depot. The narrow gauge of the Carson & Colorado ran through Sour Spring. From there, a man could ride the thirty-five-pound rails to connect with either the Las Vegas & Tonopah line to the south or double-back north to the Southern Pacific.

It's a hell of a thing, Shiloh thought, railroads crossing the country like a steel cobweb. A man on a horse, even a decent horse, doesn't stand a sinner's chance in hell against a man with a ticket.

He had another day's ride to Sour Spring. Dead tired by late afternoon, he bedded down in the meager shade of a rocky arroyo.

It was going on dusk when he rode into town. There wasn't much to Sour Spring. Built with new lumber and old canvas, Sour Spring had drawn men from as far away as Gold Hill and as close as Candelaria. Maybe they'd find gold or silver, but more than likely they wouldn't. It didn't take much more than a rumor anymore to send men packing or to build a town.

Only the train depot was built of brick.

He tied the buckskin to a rail in front of the depot and went inside. A small plump clerk dozed in the waning heat, green eyeshade pulled low over his eyes. He was leaning far back in a creaking chair, listening to the buzzing of a lonely fly against a pane of windowglass—listening to it as if that fly was the most interesting thing in the world.

"I'm looking for someone," Shiloh said, approaching the single-caged counter.

"Some fella in particular, or just anyone will do?" the clerk asked without looking up. Shiloh figured that maybe the clerk found the back of his eyeshades pretty interesting too.

"Sort of tall, thin," Shiloh answered.

"Gotta do better than that, son," the clerk said. He looked up over the eyeshades now, giving Shiloh a dubious stare. There was a combination shotgun and rifle resting across his clean counter, held by a man covered in dust with a bandana tied on his head.

"Has a cut across his head," Shiloh tried. "Appears to be a hardcase. Could be spending money in town."

"Would he be coming or going?" the clerk asked, his tone softened by the gun across his counter. "Those are the only kind I ever meet. Coming or going."

"He'd be going," Shiloh tried. "Yesterday or this morning."

"Nope, haven't seen him," the clerk said.

"You sure of that?"

"Haven't sold a ticket in three days," the clerk answered with officious certainty. "Only thing that went out is a load of ore. Next train comes in tomorrow noon, goes out ten minutes later."

Shiloh picked up the rifle and headed for the door. Behind him the clerk called out, "Don't say 'thank yer,' 'good day,' ner nothing. But you come back any time you feel the need to point that gun at a railroad man."

The three saloons and one hotel in town similarly held no answers. He could try the sheriff, but the odds ran better than even that the lawman had already received the dodger offering a reward for Shiloh's hide. In another day or two, the reward could be higher. He had killed a man in front of a barroom full of witnesses, and in the eyes of the law, he was most certainly a horse thief.

In the general merchandise, Shiloh bought a new roll of bandages, then traded the rifle for a battered Winchester repeater and a box of cartridges. The eager young clerk let Shiloh change his dressing in the stock room, but would not go so far as to throw a hat into the bargain.

The nearest saloon was just opposite the general merchandise. Rifle in one hand and reins in the other, Shiloh led the buckskin across the dusty and nearly deserted street. Tying the animal to a post close to the water trough, he stepped into the slightly cooler gloom of the bar.

"You lookin' for pretty labels or something to cut the dust?" the aging bartender asked as Shiloh stepped up to the bar. He was a small, thin man, with a large mustache. There was a hint of Texas in his voice.

"Something for the dust," Shiloh said, laying the rifle across the counter.

"That's fine then,'cause that's the only kind we sell," came the fast response. "Two bits, if you got them."

Shiloh laid the coins on the counter, and the bar-dog moved quickly for the drink.

The whiskey cut the dust, cleaning out Shiloh's mouth, but didn't do anything for the pounding in his head. The second one didn't help much either. But with the third, the pounding had diminished to a throbbing dirge.

"You find that fella you was looking for before?" the bartender asked, escaping the familiar talk of the four or five regulars lined up at the other end, to pry into a stranger's affairs.

Shiloh gave the old-timer a long look, finished off the last of his whiskey and set the glass down before answering. "No."

"Ah, that's too damn bad," the bartender said, pouring another. "He a friend of yours, is he?"

A voice from behind broke in before Shiloh could answer. "That bastard, he don't have no friends."

It was too dark to see behind him in the faded bar mirror, and Shiloh let his hand slip from the full whiskey glass partway to his gun before turning.

"Do I know you, friend?" Shiloh asked, looking into the shadows to see a lone man drinking at a table. His hat was pulled down low, casting darker shadows across his face.

"You're that one they call Shiloh or some shit, ain't you?" the man replied. "Dry-gulching, back-shooter from up near Gold Hill. I hear your luck's changed. That true?"

"Boys, I don't want no trouble here," the bartender said, motioning from behind the bar. "None at all."

The stranger stood then, pushing his hat back on his head. "That's a damn shame, old-timer,'cause you got an adult portion the minute this bastard walked in," he said, hands still resting on the table.

From where Shiloh stood, he could see that the stranger was a big man, six foot or more. He was young, well under twenty-five, and dressed in a fancy leather vest and red twill shirt. He wasn't a rancher or miner, not with that Merwin-Hulbert Army revolver tied down to his leg. The square butt of the pistol protruded just enough from the tooled, cut-away holster so that Shiloh saw a good length of the ivory grips.

"I don't want no trouble, friend," Shiloh said, one hand still on the bar and the other out at his side so he could get to the Colt.

"Don't want no trouble?" the stranger said. "That the truth, the gospel truth?"

"I just came in for a little whiskey."

"That right?" the stranger said, easing himself partway around the table.

"I don't know you, friend," Shiloh said. "And I don't want no trouble." Even as he spoke, he knew he was talking more to the bartender than the stranger. Later, when the questions came, the bartender would back up Shiloh's story. The other patrons had made a cautious retreat toward the back door.

"You don't know me," the stranger said, now facing Shiloh. "But I know all 'bout you. You were kinda an inspiration like, for me. Until you turned bad. . . ."

"Who are you?" Shiloh asked. He could feel it then, like a strong cold wind thrumming across a tight new section of Glidden wire. Like electricity running through the telegraph lines, it came down from his head, spreading out across his chest, to his arms and fingers. Then something shifted inside him, forcing his weight down through his gut to his legs and through to his boots that stood motionless on the rough-hewn flooring.

Even with his hands out to the side, he could damn well *feel* the Colt in its holster, its butt set out from the leather just so, each shining cartridge snug in its cylinder.

"You're looking kinda funny, *friend*," the stranger said, in a voice that had lost most of its bravado. "Scared?"

Shiloh could see the gunman clearly now. He could see the minute lines of the twill shirt, the small silver buttons of the black vest, and his eyes, slightly squinting in the shadows, darting nervously—left to right, then back again to Shiloh. But most of all, Shiloh could see the hands. They were shaking, one hovering out from the ivory grip. The kid wasn't anywhere near ready for what he had started, but it was too late.

"Who are you?" Shiloh repeated softly, barely moving his lips. He spoke in a whisper, his voice mechanical and flat.

The kid's eyes shifted nervously; Shiloh could see the fear rising up in them. The youngster was doing his best to fight it back down.

"Who are you?" Shiloh asked again.

From somewhere inside him, the young shootist reined in the fear. "I'm the reason your momma cried when you left home!" The last words came in a rush as the kid went for his gun.

Shiloh cleared leather, feeling his shoulder drop slightly and feet shift. He pulled the trigger without even thinking about it. The blast punched the kid back against the wall, gun hand flying up and away from his body.

He hung on the wall like a coat on a hook. A neat bullet hole between chest and stomach began to bleed down to his belt buckle. His eyes were opened wide in dull surprise, staring between the gray-blue gunsmoke that hung between the two men.

"You shot me," the kid moaned, still up against the wall. "You fast bastard."

Then the youth brought his hand down. Shiloh watched stone-faced as he struggled to level the gun on him. When the kid's trembling gun hand dropped the barrel down to head level, Shiloh shot him again.

The second shot hit him close to the first, punching him back against the wall again. The gun fell from his hand, hit the edge of the table, then clattered to the boards. Then the youth slid down the wall, legs awkwardly out in front of him.

"Goddamn, that was some fine shooting," the old-timer cackled from behind the bar. "You gave him every chance. Every chance in the world to back off. Haven't seen anything so fine since Fort Dodge, fifty or fifty-two! But you gave him every chance! He had every chance in the world."

Shiloh holstered the Colt smoothly as he turned from the body to his whiskey, knowing the truth, that the kid had no chance at all. Not a Chinaman's chance. It was the second man he had killed in a saloon in as many days, and Shiloh was damned tired of it.

The sheriff arrived a few minutes later. He was a younger version of the bar-dog, right down to the mustache. He was tall and wiry, with a rancher's deeply lined face and sun-blasted eyes. He took a long look at the kid and then pulled an Ingram watch from his vest to check the time.

"It was a fair fight," the bartender put in, first thing.

"I don't doubt it," the sheriff said. "Out of jail at noon, dead at six-thirty. Must be some kind of record."

"This fella here was drinking, peaceful like, and that youngster started in on him," the bartender continued.

"I hear ya, Zeb. Now let me get on with my job and talk to this fella," the sheriff said, turning back to Shiloh.

"It was a fair fight, I'll swear to it on a mile of Bibles," the old bar-dog persisted. "He's the fastest gun I ever seen in this two-bit deadfall."

"Zeb," the sheriff barked, looking over his shoulder, "ya quit with that or I'll take a mind to arrest *you*!"

The bartender quieted down then, moodily occupying himself by arranging his bottles.

"What ya doing in town?" the lawman asked, returning his attention to Shiloh.

"Passing through," Shiloh replied.

"Through to where?"

"South, Texas, maybe," Shiloh said.

"Drifting?" The prospect did not improve the sheriff's spirits. "Not that it matters much, but ya got a name?"

"Proffitt," Shiloh said. "Hank Proffitt."

"That boy," the sheriff said, indicating the dead man, "his name was Lyle Cowper. You know him? He was from Lawrence, Kansas."

"No, sir," Shiloh answered, looking the lawman dead in the eye.

The lawman stepped over to the dead boy, picked up the ivory-handled pistol, tested its weight, and set it on the table. "He wasn't a bad one," he said at last. "But he wanted to be."

Shiloh didn't reply, there was nothing to say.

"I locked him up last night," the sheriff continued. "Drunk and disorderly. He had that gun, a big ole Henry rifle, a Colt New Line with walnut grips, a pearl-handled hideaway, and a Creedmore, locked in a wood case."

"Any particular reason you're telling me this, Sheriff?" Shiloh asked, suddenly feeling uncomfortable under the lawman's steady gaze.

"Like he was fixin' to fight a war," the sheriff said. "Said he was looking to get into the bounty hunter or stock detective business. Asked if we got a stock association, shee-it. Ranchers round here needed him like they needed heel-flies."

"Sheriff, are you arresting me?" Shiloh asked.

"Mr. Henry Proffitt, I reckoned ya wanted to know 'bout the man laying dead over there."

"I knew enough about him," Shiloh replied. "I knew he drew down on me."

"Know what else he had in his gear with all those fancy guns?" the sheriff said, letting his gaze go from Shiloh to the corpse. "Had 'bout a dozen Buntlines. All wrapped up neat as ya please with a string. First thing, before breakfast, he was asking for one. Sat up reading it 'til I kicked him loose."

Shiloh remained quiet. Anything he said was likely to rankle the lawman.

"Shee-it," the sheriff said at last, "if it weren't ya it woulda been someone else."

Shiloh finished the drink the bartender had poured him and looked back at the lawman. "You take that boy to raise, Sheriff?"

"No, I didn't," the lawman answered. "Just don't like dead boys in my town. And while we're at it, I don't care a whole lot for strangers who are faster than decent people should be with a gun, neither."

"He's plenty quick, Sheriff," the bartender put in. "Quickest I seen in a long spell."

"Let's just see how quick he is at getting out of town then," the sheriff said, turning his back on Shiloh and walking to the door.

21

SHILOH WAS STILL at the bar when two deputies came in and hauled the body of Lyle Cowper from Lawrence, Kansas, up off the floor and out the door. The bar was still empty as Shiloh and the bartender watched.

When the batwings swung shut, the bartender poured Shiloh a fresh whiskey. "That one there is on the house," he said.

A few drinkers drifted in then, and the old-timer went over to serve them. But he returned to Shiloh straightaway. "How long you been on the dodge?" he asked, speaking in a confidential whisper as he leaned over the bar.

"I'm just passing through," Shiloh replied, sipping the top off his drink.

"Hell you are, just passing through," the bar-dog cackled. "You're running sure as I'm standing here. Sheriff, he knows it too, just doesn't want no trouble. Thirty-two dollars a month ain't nearly enough coin to deal with real trouble. And that dead boy wasn't lyin' when he said you were an adult portion."

"Like I said, I'm looking for this fella," Shiloh answered, keeping his voice low.

"That Lyle fella, he called ya by a different name," the bar-dog said. "That happens, I seen enough of it. Fellas passing through towns so fast, sometimes they leave their proper names behind. An' I reckon that a man with powder burn on his face like ya got, maybe has more reason than most."

"My name's Proffitt," Shiloh answered. "Just like I told the sheriff."

"What about that other, what the boy called you? What was that one, *Shit Toe*?"

"Shiloh," Shiloh corrected. "Some folks call me that."

"Son, there ain't no call to play cagey with me," the bartender said. "I can help ya. If the law got a dodger circulating on ya, don't ya think the sheriff's gonna be looking for it? Could be looking for it now."

Shiloh finished his whiskey, then said, "And you can help with that?"

The old-timer wrapped the bar good with one gnarled hand, and said "Hell yes, son, there ain't nothing that ain't for sale in this town. An' it helps a person to know the askin' price."

"Keep talking," Shiloh said.

"I can tell ya how much it'll cost for the sheriff ta lose a dodger, burn it, or take it out back with him when he's in the mind for a sit down."

Pushing his glass forward, Shiloh watched the old-timer pour another whiskey. "Seems to me, for a man in that position, it would cost more than what the reward is."

"See now, there ya are!" the old man exclaimed gleefully. "There's just exactly where ya wrong. Don't feel bad, 'cause ya wouldn't be the first to take that notion. But an official reward don't mean jack shit to a man who can't collect. Say fer instance, 'cause he got a price on his head too."

Shiloh drank the whiskey down in a swallow. "The sheriff?"

"Exactly correct, son," came the cheerful answer. "Long time ago in Laramie, but he still don't 'preciate no federal marshals or such coming in. What he don't own a piece of in this town ain't worth owning, poker to whores to whiskey. Everyone pays the law. Me included."

"Say if a man had a five-hundred-dollar reward on his head?"

The bar-dog wrinkled his brow, twitched his mustache, thinking. "Well sir, that might cost him twenty-five dollars."

"Well, I'm obliged then," Shiloh said, paying for the whiskey, then turning to leave the bar.

"I would reckon a fella like yourself, should be three dollars obliged," the bar-dog said with a smile.

When Shiloh turned back, hand already in his pocket, to face the bartender, the old-timer was smiling broadly. And for just an instant, in the trickery of the saloon's uneven light, the old bar-dog looked just like the professor.

There was a café across the street and Shiloh was hungry. He was stepping off the boards, thinking of selling the buckskin and saddle for twenty-five dollars, when he heard her. She didn't so much speak as grunt.

He stood perfectly still for a long moment, then turned back toward the saloon. And there, wrapped in a red Navajo blanket from ankles to neck, was Juliet Smallwater. She was sitting on a loafer's bench, feet drawn up, and giving Shiloh a look that held enough hate to curse him, her fate, the town, and every man, woman, child, and chicken in it. But even seeing that, Shiloh knew that those dark piercing eyes still held enough hate for the rest of the world.

"You just keep walking," she said at last.

"Been in town long?" Shiloh asked, moving closer.

"Long enough to see them carry a dead man from the saloon, then see you walking out a bit after."

Shiloh took another step forward.

"Just stay away, hear me?" she said.

"I figure I owe you," Shiloh replied.

"Like you owed the old man?" the girl said.

A stranger passed then, and Shiloh and the girl fell silent. When the stranger was safely inside the saloon, Shiloh asked, "You haven't seen that thin one? I had an idea he'd pass through here."

"You ain't got the brains god gave a grasshopper," the girl said. "Or is it that you just like killing?"

"You saw him, didn't you?" Shiloh insisted. He didn't know why, but he was certain that she had. "You saw that thin sonofabitch."

"I'll tell you who I saw," the girl shot back. "I saw a sheriff so crooked, they're gonna have to screw him into the ground. I saw him take my horse, saddle, and fifty dollars I had in trade for this blanket. Then I saw him put a pistol to my head and lay me down on a bunk. The bastard laughed when he gave me back the knife."

Shiloh took a step closer. He was standing over the girl now.

"I saw a fat, one-legged whore, no sober man would bed"— the girl spat—"looking to work me for three dollars a week. And the sheriff takin' half a that."

"Where is he?" Shiloh asked, his voice stone hard.

"I seen all kinds," the girl said quickly. She seemed to sink further into the blanket as she talked. "I seen your kind. You ain't dumb, but you're bad crazy. Ever see a poisoned dog, the way it'll gnaw an' tear at its own belly,'til it's gnawing at its guts. That's what you are, a damn dog that can't wait to start in at chewing on itself."

The rage was coming up in him now. A foul black thing, it rose from somewhere inside Shiloh. He was trembling with it, hands reaching for the girl.

"He's out there," she said finally, jerking her head to the north. "I saw him this morning. His horse turned up lame, he's leading it."

"Did he see you?"

She was cowering far down in the blanket, only the top part of her head was visible in the dim light. "No, I cut wide around," she said. "He had no more sense of direction than any white man."

"How long?" Shiloh asked. "When will he get here?"

She had regained some of her courage now. Her voice was once again a challenge. "If he makes camp tonight, then tomorrow," she said.

He could feel the rage leaving him, even before she finished speaking. It drew back inside, like a snake slithering into the shade of a rock. When he spoke to the girl, his voice was softer. "When tomorrow?"

"First light," the girl said. "Maybe a little after. You think you could hold off killing any more men till then?"

Shiloh turned from the girl and walked toward the café. He was four or five steps into the street when he turned again. "You eat?" he asked the girl.

"Not since morning," came the wary reply.

"Then you follow me over," he answered, waiting for her.

"That Swede lady ain't gonna let me through the damned door," came the answer.

"Then you eat in the back. Food tastes the same no matter where you put it into your mouth."

"That would be nice to find out," the girl replied, drawing herself up off the bench.

The girl was right, of course. The Swede who ran the café wouldn't have let the Indian sit down proper. But she welcomed Shiloh with a fast grin and much chatter. There were two or three men in the café—merchants, Shiloh guessed—wearing mail-order suits and derby hats.

He ordered steak and biscuits, then told the Swede to send the same out to Juliet Smallwater. After his steak came, he

wasn't three bites into it when he heard the commotion. There
was a cursing and a clatter, and then Shiloh was up out of his
seat and through the heat of the kitchen.

The girl was on the back porch facing down the big Swede,
who was nearly twice her size. She held her knife in one hand
and a tin plate in the other. As far as Shiloh could see, the
plate held nothing but a pool of gray grease, already congealing
around four small fat trimmings.

"There a problem?" Shiloh asked, staring the Swede in
the eye.

"She donta like the food," the Swede complained.

"I wouldn't feed this to a hog," the girl offered, pushing the
plate under Shiloh's nose.

"You bring her a proper steak," Shiloh said. "If I'm paying,
I want what I'm paying for."

The Swede's husband appeared then in the doorway. He was
a thin balding man with rolled-up sleeves.

"You fetch her a proper steak," Shiloh repeated, this time to
the husband.

"Feelty Indian, no steak," the little man said, waving a large
Navy revolver around nervously. "Donta cook fer no feelty
Indian."

"You know who I am?" Shiloh asked.

"That fella, who shot da boy," the woman answered in a
fading lilt.

Shiloh brought his gun hand down to the holstered Colt
before answering again. "That boy had no chance at all. You
figure that you got a better one?"

There was a quick exchange in Swedish, then the woman
disappeared through the kitchen door. When she returned, she
had Shiloh's plate in one hand and another plate in the other.
For an instant it looked like she might try something, but then
she left. The man followed her back into the kitchen, cursing
in Swedish and English.

"Crazy damned white-eyed bastard," the girl said, lowering
herself to the step.

Shiloh sat down next to her and began eating. This time he
got maybe two bites into his mouth before he felt the cold steel
of the sheriff's shotgun at the back of his head.

Shiloh froze in mid-chew.

"Damn ya boy," the lawman said, staring down at Shiloh
and raising the shotgun's barrel a notch so that it was right at

the center of his skull. "Ya can go off an' shoot some stranger from Kansas, that's one thing. It ain't a good thing, but I can live with it if you can. But when ya start pointing a gun at my cook, well sir, I feel obliged to say something."

The girl made a move, slowly shifting her hand from the plate to inside the folds of the blanket.

"Ya bring anything more than five fingers out from there, and both of ya are dead," the sheriff drawled, moving the Whitney double-barrel from Shiloh to the girl.

Juliet Smallwater withdrew her hand from the blanket as the sheriff stepped around the pair and down the stairs. He kept the shotgun swinging from one to the other as he moved.

"Now me and this squaw, we done our business," the sheriff said, crouching in front of Shiloh. "But me and you, we got some talking to do."

"How much?" Shiloh asked.

The sheriff pushed his black hat back on his head, like a man thinking. "Two hundred should take care of it."

"I got two dollars in my pocket, Sheriff," Shiloh replied.

A deep frown creased the lawman's face. "I reckon yer just shit out of luck then."

"I got that buckskin out front with a three-quarter single rig."

"Keep going," the lawman coaxed.

"Nowhere else to go," Shiloh replied.

"I seen a repeater back inside," the sheriff said. "A man that leaves a gun lying around can't be too fond of it."

"Take it."

"And while we're on the subject," the lawman mused, "that Colt on yer hip, that should even us up."

"You don't take the Colt," Shiloh answered slowly. "Take the horse, the rig, the rifle. You can take the two dollars in my pocket. The Colt stays where it is."

"Ya talk kinda brave for a man with the law's shotgun at his head," the sheriff offered.

"You go ahead then, Sheriff," Shiloh said, staring the lawman down. "You go ahead and blow my head back into that kitchen. 'Cause if you do anything less, then you'll die, right here."

"Damn." The sheriff chuckled suddenly, then turned to the girl. "He's got more guts than you could hang on a fence."

22

SO IT'S FINALLY come to this, Shiloh thought bitterly. If this is where the trail ends, then it's been a sucker's game from the first card.

Shiloh and the Indian walked down Sour Spring's one sorry, darkened street. They were heading for the rail station, where the girl said they could sleep. The saloons were lit bright, casting a yellow light out across the boards to the street, where hitched horses dozed with tipped-up feet and twitched the unseen gnats from between their ears. Beyond the painted glass and batwings came the sound of laughter and the tinny sound of a hurdy-gurdy's piano.

The pair walked by in silence, Shiloh setting his eye beyond the new-wood walls, where men were measuring out their coins in whiskey, whores, and nickel cigars. Bar-dogs were pouring with a smile, and the women were laughing and teasing. Shiloh had envied Brady's life, his sharp-tongued wife, and grassy piece of happiness.

Now, Brady and his wife were dead, and the place that seemed an Eden paradise was just another deeded section, rendered down by death to dirt and weeds, timber and water. It could be bought for a fair and proper price, just the same as whores and whiskey. The same as tobacco and papers that left a man with nothing but smoke.

"This is a goddamned life," Shiloh muttered to the girl, "where a man's gotta buy every pleasure."

The girl let out a little laugh at that and said, "That's something only a white man would think. And only a broke and stupid white man would say."

They walked in silence after that, past the last saloon on the street and last canvas and wood structure. The girl led Shiloh to an overturned Washoe wagon. He hesitated, not knowing where to turn, then she crawled under the wheel-less wagon at the rear, moving quickly, even in the blanket. Shiloh followed, his back scraping against weathered wood.

"This is the safest place," the girl said, duck-walking to the front of the abandoned wagon.

"Safest from who?" Shiloh asked, crawling forward on hands and knees.

"Safest from the law," she said, settling herself down against the wood. "From drunks, from trouble."

It was coal black under the wagon and Shiloh inched his way slowly forward.

"That's far enough," she said, when he was halfway to her.

Shiloh stopped and sat back on the fresh earth, trying to slip his arms from his coat.

"Remember that knife I got?" the girl's voice asked in the darkness.

"I recall it," Shiloh answered, folding his coat into a pillow.

"An inch farther in this direction," she said, "and you'll do more than recall it."

Shiloh lay down in the cool darkness, but could not sleep. He turned his thoughts from Brady, from the law, and the strange trail that had led him to his sorry state, but he could not cool the fever that burned in his brain.

Even as he tried to see himself with a pocket full of gold coins, rolling a Gold Flake smoke and sipping whiskey, he could not rest. It was like the fever of a sickness that worsens with the night. He turned his mind to the memory of a pretty whore's soft bed and smooth arms. He could remember it all. The way she set her tiny foot, slightly turned, against the crib's cracked doorframe, boot half unbuttoned. The thin, stooped shoulders inside the torn and yellowing lace of her shift. And the small, sad smile that told him she had known a better life and still remembered it.

The thought of that sad young whore would have set his heart to aching a week before. But now he felt nothing. He probed his heart like a bad tooth and found nothing but a numbing cankerous hate. The murderous thoughts returned. They were pictures behind his eyes that would likely send a man to madness if he looked too long. His brain churned hot with murder, but not the cunning killing that fears a judge or a hangman's rope.

Shiloh tried to cast his mind beyond the killing, but could not. Finally, in the cool and quiet darkness, he surrendered himself up to the sickness. He gave into it, just as some men surrender themselves to love, or gold, or ambition.

He stared out into the night, waiting for the blue light of dawn. When it came, he saw the depot at the end of the street and the glint of the narrow-gauge rails. The cool dun-colored earth, and the scrub beyond. Crawling on hands and knees, he emerged into the new day, like an animal leaving its foul-smelling hole. He felt neither hunger nor the fatigue of a sleepless night.

There was a horse trough up near the street for the dray animals. Shiloh drank from it, pushing his head through the night's coating of dust, far down into the warm, stagnant water. Then he straightened, shaking himself like a dog.

"My, how the mighty have fallen," the voice said, behind him. Shiloh turned to see the plump stationmaster, nickel-plated Ingersoll in hand, smiling as he made his way down the street. "Walk in yesterday all high and mighty, pointing guns at railroad employees. My oh my, how the mighty have fallen!"

Shiloh wiped the water from his face with the filthy sleeve of his coat, then drew down on the fat little man with the other.

Even in the half-light, the stationmaster could see the look in Shiloh's eye; more than the drawn Colt, this is what sent him edging his way backward across the boards.

"Me and the railroad, we don't want no problem, mister," the plump little man said in a quavering voice. It was as if Shiloh now held the C & C's own Darius Mills and all his boiled-shirt minions under the cocked hammer of the Colt.

"I'm not offering you or the railroad any problem," Shiloh answered, easing the gun back into its holster.

"He's a crazy person," the stationmaster stammered then, pointing and talking to a spot somewhere over Shiloh's shoulder. Turning, Shiloh saw the girl, still wrapped in the blanket, blinking the sleep from her eyes and looking grim as she emerged from the alley.

"He's a crazy person," the fat railroad man repeated, the fat watch still dangling from its cloth bob, all but forgotten.

Juliet Smallwater shrugged beneath the worn blanket, turned her back to Shiloh and the stationmaster, and walked. The two men watched, then Shiloh took off after her at a trot.

"Don't follow me," the girl said, quickening her step. "Pulling a gun on a railroad man. Were you thinking of stealing his watch or robbing the train?"

Shiloh fell in beside her as they made their way down the boards. "You told me dawn," Shiloh said. "That he'd be in town by sunup."

The girl stopped dead in her tracks and turned to face Shiloh. "What is it you think you are to me?" she hissed. "You think I owe you something for buying me a forty-cent supper? You got the old man killed back there. It ain't nobody's but your fault I'm broke and running from the law." She didn't look mean or hard anymore. Now she looked tired and scared.

"Maybe I can help," Shiloh said, realizing she was right.

"You?" she said contemptuously. "You're broke, running from the law, and crazy!"

"Where you headin' then?" he asked.

She had begun walking again. "Gonna find a preacher," she called over her shoulder. "A Quaker family would be best, but I'd settle for a Methodist preacher. I got a better than even chance for breakfast with either one."

Shiloh turned back toward the desert then. The girl would find her way, even in a town like Sour Spring.

He was halfway down the street, heading for the train station. The stationmaster hurried along, casting worried looks over his shoulder at the crazy man following him.

Shiloh did not know how the man would appear. A dark speck most likely, growing slowly larger in the morning light. So intent was his gaze to the north, past the stationmaster and depot, that Shiloh did not hear the sheriff's boots across the boards until the lawman was almost on him.

"Ah, pretty day," the sheriff said, falling in step beside Shiloh, the twin barrels of the shotgun lying carelessly across one arm. But not too carelessly, Shiloh suspected, as both were pointed directly at his head. The lawman's finger was on the trigger.

"Real nice, Sheriff," Shiloh replied.

"Generally I'm not up and about at sunup," the lawman said, and yawned. "By the time I get done arresting drunks and such, daylight's not too far off and I like to sleep 'til noon."

"They say it's the best part of the day."

"For sodbusters and ranchers maybe," the sheriff said. "Me, I like to sleep 'til noon. And most days I get my way.

"The days I don't, it's 'cause of some foolishness," the lawman continued, putting a meaty hand on Shiloh's shoulder and forcing him back against the front of a building. "Like take today, just for example."

Shiloh could see that both of the shotgun's hammers were pulled back. The sheriff still held the shotgun casually, right under Shiloh's chin. The other hand he planted firmly on Shiloh's shoulder, pinning him to the wall.

"Today, I had a store clerk pounding at my door 'cause someone went and pulled a gun on a railroad man."

Shiloh turned his head down the street, toward the desert, ignoring the shotgun at his jaw. Off in the distance, beyond the depot, a shadow stirred. Shiloh squinted out, but could see nothing more.

The sheriff leaned forward a little, digging his fingers into Shiloh's shoulder and bringing the shotgun up so that it tilted Shiloh's head back a little. "Now, I want ya to listen. There's a mule over at the livery. Blind as a bat, but that won't make no difference,'cause ya can see for both of ya. And there's a jug of water and three biscuits. The store clerk is setting them out now."

Far off, the shadow moved again.

The sheriff let his thumb ease one of the hammers down, then clicked it back to get Shiloh's attention. "Are you listening, boy? 'Cause this is important. The most important thing in your life."

"I hear you, Sheriff," Shiloh answered without turning his head to face the lawman.

"That's good," the sheriff said. "Because what you're gonna do is get on that blind mule, with the water and biscuits, and ride. North, south, east, or west. But you're gonna show this town your back."

"We had a deal?" Shiloh asked, squinting off into the desert. The shadow had vanished behind a stand of scrub.

"That deal was off when ya started pointing guns at railroad men," came the answer. "I want ya to think on this, ya could die right here. Right now."

"Been thinking about that reward, Sheriff?"

"Hell no," the lawman said quickly. "I been thinking about trouble and sleeping 'til noon."

Off in the horizon, the shadow took shape. It was a man leading a horse. Shiloh could feel his heart pounding at the thought, every muscle in his body stiffened. In half an hour or less, the man would reach the station platform.

"Ya listening to me, boy?" the sheriff growled.

Shiloh didn't answer, his eyes fixed on the horizon. But then he made to leave, pushing the lawman's hand off his shoulder.

The sheriff brought the scattergun's barrels down, then up fast. The top four inches caught Shiloh across the throat, forcing him back against the building. Even before Shiloh's hands were up to his neck, the lawman had stepped back. He turned the gun smoothly in a blur of blue steel and black walnut, then brought the butt smashing across Shiloh's rib cage. The blow doubled Shiloh over. As he strained, gasping for air, the sheriff reached over with one hand and grabbed the Colt neatly out of its holster, clearing leather as Shiloh came unsteadily upright.

The lawman was faster than any lazy man had a right to be. Tucking the Colt in his belt, he brought the shotgun forward again, this time hitting Shiloh high in the chest and pinning him straight up against the wall.

When Shiloh looked up, the double eyes of the scattergun were staring back, an inch or so from his nose. "Didn't I tell you, boy? I weren't lyin' to ya."

Shiloh didn't answer; he could breathe again, but painfully.

"Well, didn't I tell ya?" the sheriff insisted, holding the shotgun with one hand, butt resting in the crook of his arm. "Ya answer me, now. I ain't playin' with ya."

"You told me," Shiloh muttered, looking past the double-barrel to the mountains.

"Damn right, I told ya true," the sheriff insisted, then slapped Shiloh with a backhand blow that sent his head snapping sideways.

"Just let me get out there," Shiloh said. "I don't need any mule."

"Shit, damn me to hell on a handcar if I didn't give ya every chance," the lawman said, lowering the gun's barrels to steadily push Shiloh's neck back against the wall. He kept pushing until Shiloh could no longer breathe.

The cool metal of the barrels choked off whatever Shiloh might have said next. If the sonofabitch sheriff pulls that trigger, my head'll land right at my boots, he thought.

"Damn me if I didn't try to help ya," the lawman continued. He released the pressure on the gun some, then spit right in Shiloh's face.

The sheriff brought the gun away then. But when Shiloh made to wipe away the spit that now ran thickly down his cheek and chin, the lawman pushed his hand back down with the shotgun.

"That'll remind ya who's holding the gun," the sheriff said. "Now ya bring those hands up and come along with me."

When Shiloh turned, he felt the sheriff lift the back end of his coat and slip the Sheffield out of its sheath. Then, with the shotgun pointed at Shiloh's back, the Colt tucked into his belt, the sheriff prodded Shiloh off down the street.

"Ya just keep looking in front," the sheriff ordered, nudging Shiloh along with the greener. "There isn't nothing off in that desert that's more important to ya than walkin' straight and doing like I say."

There was a true horror in it, and Shiloh could see it unfolding as the sheriff led him away. Despite his threat, Shiloh knew the sheriff would not shoot him in the middle of the street. There would be questions to answer that way. The sheriff would ride him out of town and make him dig his own grave.

Brady's killer would be walking into town even as the sheriff began covering the body. The killer would have money in his pocket. The whores and bartenders would treat him right. The sheriff would treat him right. And then he would ride off on a fresh horse and a new saddle.

They were in the center of town, the sheriff walking a pace or two behind Shiloh, howdying folks who were coming out on the boards as they made their way past saloons and storefronts.

"What you got there, Sheriff?" someone called.

"Just a fella who don't act right round decent people," came the happy response. "Gonna show him the city limits. Point him up to Gold Hill where they're used to such foolishness."

When they reached the livery, the sheriff nudged Shiloh into the darkened barn and closed the wide doors after them. "See that there?" he said, tapping the shotgun on Shiloh's right shoulder to make him look. There in a middle stall was a mule, already harnessed.

"I don't need the mule," Shiloh said, his head clearing from the hate. "Just hand back my gun and let me walk west."

The sheriff nudged Shiloh forward into the hay-smelling shadows. "Damn right, ya don't need no mule. Boy, we done passed that fence. And that was your choice."

Then the shotgun pushed hard against Shiloh's back. He waited for the blast that would cut him in two. But instead, there came a wheezing sound as the sheriff fell forward, one hand clawing up Shiloh's shoulder as the greener's barrels came up across his ear.

Turning on his boot heel and slapping his side for a gun that wasn't there, Shiloh saw Juliet Smallwater, knee braced in the small of the lawman's back, twisting her knife in the base of his skull. The thin blade was buried to the hilt as she gave it another quick half-turn, then withdrew it in one smooth pull. Shiloh noticed that she was smiling as she carefully cleaned both sides of the blade across the lawman's ear, stropping it back and forth like a barber.

There were two holes in the sheriff. One in the back, where she had plunged the knife through to his lung, and the other she had taken her time with, stabbing straight up through the opening in the base of his skull.

"I guess I owe you," Shiloh said, reaching down to retrieve his Colt and knife from under the dead man.

"You think I did that for you?" came the disgusted reply. "If he had that scattergun cocked, your miserable hard-luck guts *would be* hanging on a fence."

The girl went through the lawman's clothes, looking for her fifty dollars and cursing each item that she brought out. All she found was ten dollars, a new Barlow knife, and a blue poker chip. Shiloh guessed that the poker chip had been the lawman's lucky charm.

She pocketed the ten dollars, offering Shiloh only a challenging stare to discourage any thought of an even split. "The owner's gonna be back soon," she said. "The town's gonna think you did it."

Shiloh slipped the Sheffield back into its sheath, then checked the load in the Colt. "In an hour, it won't matter any," he replied, turning toward the door.

"You walk out that door, and it won't matter in ten minutes," she called when his hand was on the latch. "They'll kill you.

Sheriff takes a man into a stable with a shotgun at his back, they don't expect to see that fella walk out alone. Or me neither. And don't go thinking 'bout the back way. That's where the stable man's working at a harness."

23

IT WAS THE girl's idea, and a good one at that. After tying the livery owner up with a length of harness, Shiloh led the blind mule, with the girl astride, through the stable's double doors and down the middle of Sour Spring's one street.

They were a strange sight, to be sure. So strange that shop-keepers, clerks, bar dogs, and loafers crowded the boards to watch the pair pass. They laughed openly, pointing and calling to each other across the dusty street. But none of them pulled a gun. The two were nothing but a bit of distraction on a dull day. No one thought to ask after the sheriff, who was lying dead in an empty stall.

The girl did not climb down from the mule until they arrived at the train depot. A few wagons were tied up at the post, and a dozen loafers sat along the benches and in the shade of the platform, waiting for the train. Some were waiting for supplies, others mail. But most gathered at the depot to watch the train pull in, take its fill of water, and then pull out again. It wasn't much, but that was about all that Sour Spring offered in the way of excitement. And for most, it was plenty.

"He isn't here yet," Shiloh said, looking around the plat-form. No, he wasn't there, but he would arrive shortly. Shiloh half expected to meet him on the street as they were lea-ving town.

Then they heard the train—first the nearing whistle, then the engine, and then the whistle again as it pulled in. Shiloh trotted around the depot as the girl climbed down from the mule. Loafers and men who'd been dozing in the wagons stretched and rose, making their way around to the platform.

The small engine and half dozen cars came squealing and clanking to a tortured stop that blocked Shiloh's view of the desert, but he could *feel* the gunman out there. He would be close now, almost close enough for Shiloh to see his face.

Shiloh would walk around the train and across the tracks to meet the sonofabitch. And in ten minutes it would be over.

He moved fast now, walking through the hissing steam, feeling the heat of the engine's boilers. Shiloh was nearly halfway down the line of cars when he saw them. The fat stationmaster was helping two Pinkertons down from the coach car. They could be nothing else, in their dark, newly brushed suits and crisp hats. Each carried a cased rifle and warbag. Their clean-shaven faces and careful dress seemed absurd.

To the plump stationmaster, Shiloh must have looked like a vision from that special corner of hell reserved for railroad employees. The stationmaster watched in horror as Shiloh emerged through a cloud of steam, hand on his pistol and a muderous look in his eyes.

The fat man fell back in a stoop, nearly tripping one of the Pinks as he pulled the stool away with him. Surely, the fat stationmaster thought that the crazy man had returned to cold-bloodedly murder a faithful C & C employee.

Then Shiloh was past them, the stationmaster and the two Pinkertons. Someone behind him was yelling, but he kept walking. When he reached the last car, he cut across the tracks at a trot, boots crunching down the cinders.

"Hey, you!" someone called, but his voice was drowned out by the two sharp blasts from the train's whistle.

When he reached the other side of the train, Shiloh could see him. Brady's killer was farther down the tracks, near the water tower. He was leading the lame horse, just as the girl had said.

The train was moving then, and Shiloh was right alongside it.

"Hey! Hey!" came the cry at his back, but Shiloh kept moving.

Then the killer turned. He wasn't more than a hundred yards off. For the briefest instant he stopped, his attention drawn by the shouts. Shiloh cleared leather, drawing down on the thin man as the lame horse hobbled forward, neatly blocking the view.

Cursing, Shiloh lowered the Colt, and moved toward the killer at a run, his long strides matching the movement of the train that labored alongside as it made its way to the water tower.

Then there was a hand on his shoulder, a big powerful paw that nearly knocked him off his feet as it spun him around.

"Hey!" the big Pink said, fingers digging into Shiloh's flesh.

Shiloh turned and brought the Colt up in one smooth motion.

"The station agent . . ." the small Pink started, but never got a chance to finish. He was too busy staring down the barrel of the Colt.

"What?" Shiloh asked, surprised at the calmness of his own voice. "I'm a mite busy here."

The train was passing them now, chugging along slowly toward the water tower, moving like a thirsty horse in the noonday heat. Shiloh moved the pistol from one Pinkerton to the other.

"Give me the guns," Shiloh ordered. When neither made a move, he reached under the nearly new suits, pulled each pistol out from its holster and tucked them into his belt.

"You Shiloh?" the larger one asked.

Shiloh didn't answer; rather, he backed off slowly from the two Pinks, Colt still raised. Then he turned quickly and began running again.

The killer had vanished. All that remained was the horse, reins dangling free around its neck. He had crossed the tracks, in front of the locomotive.

By the time Shiloh had reached the engine, the fireman was pulling the pipe around and pulling the water tower's cord.

"Hey!" one of the Pinks called again from the distance.

Shiloh turned, freezing the pair in their steps as he raised the Colt, then hustled across the tracks in front of the stopped locomotive.

There was no sign of the killer. He was most likely nearing town by now. Shiloh began running again, the Pinks' guns digging into his belly. Out of the corner of his eye, he could see the crowd at the depot's platform staring.

When he reached town, he came up on it from behind. A Chinese woman hanging laundry cursed him, saw the drawn Colt, then hurried inside. Chickens scattered. The Pinks' guns fell from his belt as he climbed a fence, but he did not stop for them.

When he came to the building he recognized as the saloon, Shiloh tried the door. Stepping into the darkened passageway, he was greeted by a room filled with busted crates and empty barrels. Beyond was the sound of hushed conversation and coins clicking down on wood. He pushed a threadbare curtain away and stepped into the hind end of the saloon.

"Well goddamn, boy," the old bar-dog said, bottle raised over a shot glass. "Goddamn."

There were four or five loafers at the bar. With the first glance at the drawn Colt they scattered, as Shiloh made his way to the front of the bar.

"Looking for a stranger," Shiloh panted, out of breath from running. "Thin one."

"You don't see him here, do ya?" the bar-dog shot back, more annoyed then scared, as he lowered the bottle. "Just keep moving. Go on, do your killing down the street."

Shiloh advanced to the bar, watching the hands of each drinker carefully, knowing that he would shoot the first one who made a sudden move. But none did; they watched the stranger carefully as he eased his way along the length of the bar toward the doors.

When he came through the batwings with his gun drawn, Shiloh moved quick, first in one direction, then the other, scaring a woman and small boy. The woman covered the boy's head with both hands and pushed him out of the way, through the saloon doors.

He worked his way into the middle of the street, gun out in front of him as he turned in a slow circle.

"Here I am, you sonofabitch!" he yelled. "You're gonna die!"

The street was clearing now. Women and men slipped into storefronts and alleys. The sound of anxious boots could be heard clearly on Sour Spring's emptying street.

"Come on, you murdering bastard!" Shiloh yelled, sighting down the Colt at every store window and doorway. Shades and curtains were drawn down from one end of the street to the other. Here and there, he could see a face peering out from a corner.

When no one answered, he walked back up on the boards. The general merchandise store had its shades drawn. Shiloh tried the locked door. When he kicked in the glass, a shotgun blast crashed through the window next to him.

"You murdering bastard, I'll send you to hell," Shiloh screamed, going to his knees as he brought the Colt up.

Inside the darkened store was nothing but silence. Reaching cautiously up with his gun hand, Shiloh tapped lightly at the front window. Another blast shattered the lettered glass, sending a spray out across the boards and into the dusty street. Before the last trickle of glass fell, Shiloh was on his feet and through the busted door. There, cowering on the floor, was the frightened young store clerk, fumbling with an opened shotgun and two shells.

"Where is he?" Shiloh demanded, drawing down on the clerk.

"Ain't nobody here, mister," the clerk replied, setting the scattergun down with shaking hands. "Mr. Culbertson, he ran out the back."

"Where is he?" Shiloh repeated, moving into the room, gun turning from left to right, sighting down on barrels of flour, large bowls of penny candy, and bolts of material.

The clerk pushed back against the counter, hands up to his face. "Mister, there ain't nobody here. Look for yourself."

Walking past the clerk, Shiloh moved warily through the back room. The door was open. Peeking out, over the Colt's barrel, he saw no one.

When he walked back through the store, he picked up the shotgun and threw it off into a corner. He was halfway out the shattered door when a rifle slug pounded into the doorframe, shaking the entire front of the store. Shiloh fired off a round without even looking. Across the street, more glass broke, and Shiloh crouched low in the darkened store. Giving a look through the shades, he saw an old man, the barber, across the street, with a big Henry. He was reloading.

"Mister," the clerk stammered, "I'd just 'preciate it like hell if you'd see fit to leave now."

"Old man across the street with a rifle," Shiloh said, working his way back toward the counter.

"That'd be Mr. Bensen," the clerk said. "Ya ain't after him, are ya? Jesus, don't go killing Mr. Bensen."

Shiloh turned on the boy, pistol up.

"Hell, shoot 'im," the boy said weakly. "I don't give no fiddler's damn."

"You don't come after me with that shotgun, I won't shoot *you*," Shiloh snapped, then eased his way back around the counter.

He was out the back door in an instant, running through unfenced yards. When he reached what he took to be the back of a saloon, he opened the door and slipped through.

Three waiter gals screamed and scattered as he entered the back end through a door covered by a beaded curtain. It was a larger saloon than the first. Faro tables, chuck-a-luck, and a wheel lined one wall. Across the room, the fancy dressed bartender bent fast, and Shiloh fired a round into the mirror above his head that brought him straight up again.

"You bring that out nice and easy now," he ordered, pulling the Colt's hammer back.

The bar-dog bent slowly, eyes glued to Shiloh. When he rose he was holding a sawed-off by the butt.

"Toss it there," Shiloh ordered, pointing down to the bar with his gun.

The bar-dog did as he was told. "We don't want no trouble," he said.

There were two or three drinkers in the bar, and Shiloh ordered them to throw down their weapons and join the bartender and waiter gals at the back of the room. They did as they were told, moving like herded sheep, hands slightly raised up in front of them.

He was nearly to the batwings when a shot exploded from behind him, sending the blue-painted door jerking slightly outward. Someone in the group had a hideaway and wasn't timid about trying it. Shiloh didn't turn to see who it was. He was through the door and back into the glare of sunlight in two steps.

Shiloh hit the boards running. A half dozen more shots sang out before he'd gone five steps. The bullets chewed into the rough boards at his heels and pounded into the buildings at his shoulders. He ran low, in a crouch, pistol up in front of him, and his head tucked down as far as he could manage.

They were shooting from the roofs, concealed by false fronts. They were shooting from darkened windows. They were aiming to shoot him down in the street like a mad dog.

He turned and fired without aiming, then fired again, looking to hold off the hidden gunmen, but each shot only triggered a hail of renewed gunfire.

As he ran, Shiloh tried the door of every building. Each door was locked. From an alleyway across the street someone fired a shotgun, letting go with both barrels at once. Shiloh felt the hot bite of bird-shot at his neck and face, like swarming hornets. The blow raised him up from his crouching run and pushed him into a faltering stumble as he reached a doorway. The thick wood of the door fell away as Shiloh tried to regain his footing, and he staggered into the room.

Slamming the door shut and bolting it, Shiloh turned to see that he was in the sheriff's office. Blood was running down his neck, he could feel it soaking into his shirt. Bringing his hand up, he painfully rolled a dozen double-O pellets into his bloodied hand, letting them fall down the front of his coat to the floor.

He was trapped.

24

SHILOH HEARD HIM even before he saw him. The sudden scrape of a chair across floorboards brought Shiloh whirling around from the door, gun in hand and leveled.

And there in the half-light of the shuttered office, sitting behind the paper-strewn desk as if he owned it, was Brady's killer. Even in the dim light there could be no mistake about it; a greasy piece of rag, soaked through with blood, covered the head wound.

The thin man was coming to his feet and fumbling for his gun. "Ya crazy bastard," was all the killer could say as he raised his hands up in front of him.

Suddenly he looked much smaller than Shiloh remembered him. It was hard to believe that such a man could have had a hand in Brady's death.

"You're gonna die, right now," Shiloh said, hearing his own voice as cold and flat as ice on a rainbarrel. Already he could feel the weight lifting. The madness would pass with one bullet.

"I didn't do nothing ta ya, mister," the man said, inching his hand back down toward the butt of his holstered pistol.

Shiloh took a step closer, moving around the desk. "Just so you know why you're dying. It's because you killed a friend of mine. Murdered him and his wife."

"I didn't kill nobody!" came the stammering answer. "Yer the one goes round shooting folks!"

"Shiloh! You in there?" someone called from the street. "This here is Briggs and Cantin from the Pinkerton Agency!"

"See there," the killer said, a smile spreading across his face. "They ain't after me. They after ya!"

"Shiloh! You come out," the Pinkerton yelled. "You'll get a fair trial. We know you killed the sheriff. We have the girl."

The killer was almost gleeful now. "See there, they gonna hang yer raggedy ass."

Shiloh raised the gun slightly, bringing the killer's hands back up, away from the tied-down holster. He could see the man's face start to sweat and twitch as he stared down the barrel of the Colt.

Shiloh thumbed back the hammer, wanting the thin man to hear it. "No matter. You're getting your trial right now." Shiloh pulled back slow on the trigger, studying the killer's face carefully. It had been a hard and bloody trail, and he wanted to watch this man die. He wanted it as badly as he had ever wanted anything in his life.

But he had been too long about it. Just before the hammer came down, the killer kicked out, sending the sheriff's chair crashing into Shiloh's shins. The shot went high, drilling into the wall above the desk. As Shiloh fell back, he fired again, but the hammer came down on a spent cartridge.

The thin man moved quick, bringing out his gun and clearing leather even as Shiloh threw the Colt forward and charged him. The Colt hit him high in the chest, and Shiloh went for the gun. He reached it in a step, pushing it up by the longbarrel, but feeling the cool steel slip from between his bloodied fingers. With his other hand, Shiloh grabbed the killer's wrist and bent it back just as his other hand slid from the barrel.

The gun went off then, deafening in the small office; Shiloh felt the killer's hand jerk with the force of it Then he had the gun by the barrel again, this time in a firm grip. Twice more the gun fired, the bullets sinking into the ceiling to release a light dusting snow of caulking.

"Shiloh, you come outa there," a Pinkerton called from the street. "Don't make it any worse on you or your squaw lady-friend."

The gunman held the pistol with two hands, grimacing with the effort as he worked the barrel down toward Shiloh's head. His finger was wrapped tightly down on the trigger, and he knew that to release the pistol to Shiloh's bloodied hand meant dying.

Shiloh grunted with the effort of turning the gun barrel back, away from his head. All the time, he looked directly into the killer's frightened eyes, wanting to see the life fade from them.

When the killer reached his full height, he struck out with his free hand, the blow catching Shiloh square in the jaw. But he didn't let up his grip. The killer hit him again, this time coming down hard across his neck. Now he could feel it, the gun slipping ever so slightly from the killer's hand.

"Sonofabitch, you're gonna die," Shiloh hissed through clenched teeth as the barrel turned toward the thin man's face.

As the gun slipped from his grasp, the killer fired off three more shots that filled the small room with powder smoke. They came fast, one after another, each one slamming into the wall. If the thin man was going to lose the gun in the struggle, he sure as hell wasn't going to have it loaded.

Then the gun came free. It slid from the killer's hand so unexpectedly that Shiloh lost his balance for a second. But a second was all it took.

The thin man let go with two quick punches to Shiloh's head. The first broke his nose, sending a spray of blood that splattered against one whitewashed wall as the muffled crack of cartilage sent a numbing pain throbbing through Shiloh's head. The second blow parted a neat section of lip and loosened a tooth, but had the thin man spitting curses when a two-inch gouge opened across his knuckle.

The force of the blows pushed Shiloh back, sending his head turning sharply and his gun hand up out to his side. The coppery, salt-tinged taste of blood filled his mouth. It flowed freely down into his throat from the busted nose and the opened wound on his lip.

The thin man fought mean. Like a starved dog, he sprang forward as Shiloh brought the pistol up. Even in the darkened room, Shiloh saw the steely flash of the Navaja jump into the killer's hand from its side sheath.

But the thin man was too anxious. Fear and animal viciousness had replaced caution as he moved in, swinging and jabbing the knife before him. Shiloh turned the gun, one-handed, so that he now held it by the barrel. And when the thin man leapt at him, he laid a savage blow across the killer's wrist that sent the knife flying from his fingers toward the back of the room and through the bars of an empty cell.

The killer grasped his wrist in a yelp of pain, and Shiloh hit him again, the blow reopening the ugly bandaged wound at the top of his head. In an instant, blood was matting down his hair and running in a dozen jagged lines down his face as he backed away.

"You're gonna die," Shiloh said, moving slowly toward the dazed outlaw, who had retreated to a corner.

The killer rubbed the blood from his eyes and rushed forward. When he hit, both feet were off the floor and the thin man's weight threw Shiloh back against the wall with a force that knocked the pistol from his hand.

The thin man was a brawler, his thumbnails long and sharpened down to yellowed points. Shiloh saw the flash of a fist at his eyes, blocked it, then brought the heel of his right hand up quick, snapping the killer's jaw shut and forcing him back a step.

The two men stood there, staring each other down, each bent low, hands out at their sides, a foot apart in the small room. Shiloh could feel his busted nose throbbing painfully, no longer good for breathing. He stood there for what seemed a lifetime, panting through his mouth. He could feel the blood drying on his face and running down his chin. When his throat filled with it, he spat, releasing a thick gout across the floor between him and the killer.

"Ya ain't lookin' so good, pardner," the killer wheezed, easing his way forward.

Shiloh didn't answer. Instead, he brought his fists up as he cut an anxious look over at the pistol that was resting against the door.

The killer followed Shiloh's gaze, smiled, and took a step closer. "I kilt them," he said at last. "I kilt them, an' now I'm gonna kill ya."

"Shiloh, you come out," a Pinkerton called from the street. "You come out, or we're coming in."

"See there, ya bastard, law's on *my* side," the killer said.

Shiloh made to reach for his own knife, but the thin man moved faster. Before he had his fingers on the handle, the killer was on him again. Those sharpened thumbnails gouged for Shiloh's eyes, opening a cut across his cheek. The other dug with a blinding pain at the side of the busted nose, grinding the uneven ends of cartilage against each other.

"This is the last warning you get!" the Pink called as Shiloh wrapped his fingers around the killer's thin neck.

Shiloh could feel his nose flattening against his cheek as the other sharpened nail struggled to gouge out his left eye.

With both hands around the thin man's scrawny neck, he worked the killer back at arm's length, the thin man's hands clawing air as his boots shuffled and strained on the boards.

Then he could feel the fight going out of the thin man. The hands stopped clawing toward Shiloh's face and dropped as the sharpened nails plunged into the back of the hands that held his throat. Shiloh could feel the pain up to his shoulders, but he kept moving the thin man, feeling the fight go from his legs. In an instant, he had the killer pinned against the shuttered window. With both hands wrapped around the killer's throat, he could see the eyes begin to bulge as his face turned a purplish crimson.

Shiloh could feel it then. A new strength rising up in him. In the half-light of the dead lawman's office, he could feel the sickness take hold as he stared into the dying man's fear-filled eyes. He drank in the killer's dying—drank it greedily down into himself like good whiskey.

Then there was a blast. A dozen inches above the thin man's strangling face a load of buckshot smashed through the window's shutters. Shiloh could feel the sting of the hot pellets and wood splinters across his face and busted nose, blinding him as a fist-sized shaft of white sunlight stabbed through the jagged hole.

Both men fell on the floor, Shiloh falling on top of the killer as he tightened his grip around the thin man's throat. But no sooner had they hit the boards than one of those sharpened nails came up to catch Shiloh under the chin, then break off with a half turn as it wedged itself between jaw bone and muscle.

The pain and force of the blow opened Shiloh's strangling fingers and sent him tumbling backward. He hit the floor on his side with an animal yell, futilely trying to claw the broken nail from his jaw, turning his fingers bloody with the effort.

The killer came to his feet coughing and was advancing on him. "I helped kill them," he gasped. "Kilt that sonofabitch Pink an' that woman."

Another shotgun blast splintered the shutter, sending a second thick shaft of sunlight into the office behind the killer. Then Shiloh could hear men at the doors, back and front. Someone was laying into the front door with an ax. In another second they would be in the office.

Shiloh went for his knife again, reaching behind him, but the thin man kicked out, catching him high across the arm and turning him onto his side.

Then he kicked again. The pointed toe of his boot caught Shiloh in the stomach and forced a gasp of air from his chest, sending another spray of blood from Shiloh's mouth and rolling him onto his back, arm bent awkwardly behind him.

"We kilt them, fancy like. Took our time 'bout it."

Through blurring eyes, Shiloh could look up beyond the killer. A hand reached tentatively in through the shotgunned shutters, blocking the dust-crowded length of sun as it searched for the latch.

Then Shiloh could feel it, the bone handle of the Sheffield pressing against his wrist like a gift. He brought his hand back an inch and tightened his fingers around the familiar grip.

"Me, I had that fine woman, twice," the killer said mockingly, bringing his boot back, the full-drop twenty-point spurs aiming for Shiloh's head. "Ya seen that Pink, it was me that done 'im up real pretty, ya bastard."

Shiloh could no longer feel the pain. He could feel nothing but the hate. Rolling to his side, he caught the killer's boot in one hand as he brought the knife out from behind his back with the other.

The killer's eyes went blank as Shiloh slashed savagely at the leg, slicing into boot leather. He slashed out again, higher now, up between the killer's legs, but missed as the man hopped back, the shotgunned shutter breaking his fall. The boot fell from Shiloh's hand as the killer danced off to the side.

"I'll tell ya' how it was," the thin man said, coming forward, once again eager for a fight.

Shiloh came to his feet, knife out and at his side as he rushed blindly toward the outlaw. They crashed backward, both of the thin man's hands holding Shiloh's knife hand upward.

"Me an' Dwight kilt them, ya bastard," the thin man hissed as Shiloh's force propelled them past the two Pinkertons and into the blinding sun of the just-opened door.

They tumbled out through the door, crashing through the line of men and across the boards. The hitching rail gave way under their weight and they fell into the street.

Shiloh broke free, coming into a half crouch as the thin man's eyes darted like a trapped animal's.

"You tell me how it was," Shiloh rasped. "Tell me before you die."

"Hold it there, boys," a voice ordered from behind them, followed by the double-click of shotgun hammers.

Shiloh paid them no mind; he advanced on the killer, his knife hand making smooth arcs in front of him. "Tell me how it was."

"Go ta hell, ya murdering bastard," came the fast response. "Ain't none a ya gonna shoot 'im?"

But nobody did.

Shiloh came in fast, slashing out and backhanded. The killer danced back a half step and stumbled. The blade caught him across the chin, opening a light gash.

"Tell me how it was," Shiloh demanded. The men weren't going to stop him. The Pinks had heard what the thin man had said about doing the killings. Now they held off the others.

"I'll tell ya in hell," the killer spat, feeling the fresh slice across his chin with a hand that came away bloody. "Ain't nobody gonna shoot this dog?"

No answer came from the gathering crowd. There was a wide circle of men now. They spilled out from the boards into the street. The boldest women inched their way forward, peeking over the shoulders of the men. Children, waist high, worked their way through, only to be pushed back. And right out in front were the two Pinkertons. They looked calm, as if they were at some bare-knuckled prizefight, but hadn't made a bet. They were the only law in Sour Spring now. Clean suits and Pinkerton badges were their only claim. But that was enough and certainly more than the dead sheriff ever had.

"Tell how it was," Shiloh whispered, the Sheffield cutting through the air.

The killer moved back as Shiloh advanced, his eyes searching the crowd, looking for help among the stony faces that stared back. No help was offered.

"You tell, mister," a voice from the crowd shouted.

Shiloh came in quick then, slashing from right to left, catching the thin man across the forehead.

The killer's eyes burned bright with hate. There was no hope in the crowd that watched, their faces eager for the blood of a killing. The world had drawn in on itself and gathered into a ragged circle of worn denim, patched shirts, dusty hats, faded gingham, and shiny mail-order suits.

Shiloh stepped in. The knife had never felt so light in his hand. His eye had never seen so clearly. "Tell me," he whispered, though the whole crowd heard.

"He's a crazy person," the thin man stammered. "Ain't nobody gonna help?"

Nobody moved to help, and the only law in Sour Spring looked on with grim, professional interest.

"Tell it," a dozen voices insisted.

"Who'd you kill?" one of the Pinkerton's asked then, his voice low and confidential, the tone of a lawman wheedling a confession.

When Shiloh lashed out again, the killer backed away, hands up in front. The blade drew two deep valleys across the palms. "Tell me."

"Me an' Dwight killed 'em," the thin man confessed, holding his bloodied hands up as he backed away. "Ain't nobody gonna stop him?"

"Who was it you killed?" the Pink asked again, holding the uncased shotgun comfortably across his arm.

The knife flew out again, this time cutting straight to the bone of the thin man's wrist. "Tell it," Shiloh spat through a mouthful of blood.

"Me and Dwight killed 'em," the outlaw screamed, holding the slashed wrist in a bloodied palm. "That Pinkerton an' 'is wife. Up near Copley."

The thin man was moving away fast now, in a stumbling retreat. When his back touched the hitching post opposite the sheriff's office, he began moving down the street. The crowd kept apace.

Shiloh lunged now, cutting the blade across the thin man's face, the bloodied blade carving out a gash across his upper lip as steel clicked against his teeth.

"Tell it."

"It was Dwight's idea."

Shiloh lashed out again, the knife's handle slick with his blood, the blade flashing across the killer's bloodied hands. "Tell it, you murdering bastard."

"All a you miserable bastards. Ya all just gonna watch? I'll see you all in hell for this," the thin man cursed.

"What'd you do, boy?" the small Pinkerton asked.

"We nailed that Pinkerton fella up to the porch. An' took turns at his wife. Made him watch."

When Shiloh sent the blade flying again, it sliced a deep groove across the killer's nose, grinding into cartilage. Then Shiloh came in again fast as the thin man's hands went up. The Sheffield's blade widened the thin man's mouth as it sliced through his left cheek to reveal a yellow line of bloody teeth peeking through the flap of flesh. It was a wound almost like Brady's and seeing it set Shiloh's mouth into a horrible, twisted smile.

"I hit 'im with an ax when it was Dwight's turn. Ta git him to tell where the money was," the killer tried through his slashed mouth. Each tortured word sent a new spray of blood forward.

Shiloh lunged in with the knife, the point cutting through the thin man's eyelid and slicing across the eye. He stumbled then, falling backward into the dust. In a flash, Shiloh jumped on him, the blade sinking through the palm of his ruined hand, which was held up in surrender, and pinning him to the center of the street, just as Brady had been nailed to the porch.

Shiloh had his hands around the killer's throat. He could feel the thin man's chest heave as he stared into the one wide-open eye, the other a bloody horror.

The crowd moved in closer to see the kill. Then a girl's voice began to shriek. "Stop it! Stop it! Stop it!"

The shriek brought Shiloh's head snapping up. He could see her, standing in the crowd. She was young, no more than fourteen or fifteen, and wearing a gray dress. Her eyes were wide, not with disgust, but terror. She was shaking from head to toe, hysterical as her fingers clawed through her blonde hair and down her face. Her mouth was twisted into a long screeching wail. Nothing in her young life had prepared her for what she saw.

"Stopitstopit!" she screamed, her voice shrill in the hushed crowd. She shook as if in a fit, her fingernails trailing deep scratches along her smooth cheeks and distorting her eyes into a grotesque mask.

The thick hands of a rancher around her shoulders eased her back from the circle. Someone else slapped her then, hard. But the screaming continued. "God, God, God, please!"

Shiloh could no longer see her, but the screaming continued. Suddenly he was aware of the insane animal smile that his mouth had formed itself into. Looking down, he could see the outlaw's own bloody and ruined face. A small stream of blood ran from Shiloh's nose and lip to add to the outlaw's bloody countenance.

"Oh, Lord, please doan," the thin man sobbed in a small voice.

"Now you're gonna die, you sonofabitch," Shiloh hissed.

And that's when the killer's head exploded in Shiloh's grasp. The world went blank in a deafening flash that left his ears numb, his fingers burning, and his eyes stinging as he blinked through the powder smoke. Before him, he saw the thin man's head blasted downward into the dust. The outlaw's head had vanished; what remained was not a man.

The evil he had hunted no longer had a face. Nothing was left but bone, and brain, and bloodied tufts of hair spread out three feet in every direction from a widening puddle of blood at its center.

Shiloh brought his trembling fingers from around the dead man's neck and turned to see the barrel of the ten-gauge that had stolen the thin man's death from his grasp. Drawing the knife from the outlaw's palm, he made to rise. The girl's distant voice still ringing shrill and hysterical in his half-deaf ears, he bent upward at the knees to face the man who had stolen his vengeance.

Then there was another flash, this one silent, as the pick handle landed across the back of his head.

EPILOGUE

SHILOH AWOKE INTO a world of pain. His body ached from one end to the other. It was the kind of pain that makes a man think of cool gun metal against his head with his own finger wrapped tight around the trigger. It drew him up from a black and dreamless sleep to a jail cell filled with blinding sunlight. As he awakened, he could hear the moaning. A tortured, dry-throated moan of the damned. Then he slowly realized that it was his own voice that echoed in the empty cell.

Two men came then, clanking open the cell door. They forced his mouth roughly open with a wooden spoon and poured the laudanum down his throat. He gagged as the thick liquid burned into his split lip, spilling out up over his chin and down his chest. Then he drank it thirstily, knowing it would ease the pain but not his thirst.

"Crazy bastard," one said.

"Crazy ain't the word," the other replied.

The door rang shut, and soon the warmth spread over him like a thick blanket. The drug sent him floating through pleasant dreams of a life long past and half-forgotten.

He dreamed of the first time he kissed a girl. He stole the kiss right out on a busy street. Her lips were both dry and cool, and she blushed mightily, right down into the lace of her starched collar. His own lips carried the memory of the brief touch for a week.

"Henry Proffitt, you're going directly to hell for that!" she declared. But she didn't run off.

Then he awoke again into the pale flicker of lantern light. And they forced more laudanum down his throat. He could feel the bandages on his face, covering his busted nose, where the shotgun blast had caught his cheek, and the place where someone had removed the killer's broken fingernail.

It was later the night chills came. Shiloh reached out in darkness for a blanket and found none. He moved, moaning with the pain, and discovered that he was naked as a jay. Through a dim memory of drugged sleep, he remembered them cutting his blood-stiffened clothes from him but could not recall a doctor's care.

Through force of will he slid one leg forward toward the edge of the bunk. There was a clink of chain and then a pull from the shackles around his ankles. Painfully testing his arms, he found his hands shackled together and secured to leg-irons by a length of chain.

Shiloh moaned out in the darkness, hearing his voice pitiful and lonely in the empty cell. But no bootsteps or lantern light came from the outer room. Folding one hand into the other, he drew his body down and placed them between his legs, waiting for sleep.

When he woke again, it was into the half-light of either dawn or dusk. The pain had lessened, but Shiloh still could not move. He lay motionless, staring at the cracked and waterstained ceiling through slitted eyes. With his brain still clouded by the drug, the country spread out before him. Railroads and rivers wound their torturous routes east to west. Valleys and towns revealed themselves in aging plaster. And he thought that it was a country so vast that a man could lose himself forever within it.

They came again, then. Shiloh watched as they lowered the brown bottle to his lips, then tilted it so that the drug ran smoothly down his throat. Once again it spread out through his arms and legs, its warmth delivering him up to a dark and painless sleep filled with pleasant dreams.

When he opened his eyes again, Juliet Smallwater was standing over him, holding a tin bowl and a spoon.

"They told me to give you soup," she said grimly.

"How long?" Shiloh managed, his mouth dry and foul tasting.

"Two days, almost three," she said, bringing the spoon with clear broth to his lips.

The soup was neither warm nor hot, but he took it quickly. He wanted to feed himself and grabbed the spoon from the girl. But his hands shook so badly he lost most of the soup. Disgustedly, she took the spoon back and finished the task.

He didn't speak again until the bowl was empty. "They gonna hang me?"

"Not that they told me," she said, rising up off the edge of the bunk. "Been working the telegraph night and day, figuring what to do with you."

Before she left, the girl unlocked the chains that held his legs to the bed. Through the slit of a window, Shiloh saw the gathering light in the sky and decided that it was near dawn.

He could stretch his legs off the bed, but not support himself. There was a slop bucket near the bed. When he used it, his piss flowed burning and bloody, then changed to a flowery shade of pink.

He fell back into the bunk then and slept. When he opened his eyes, the light had not changed, though he knew it must now be sunset.

One of the Pinkertons was standing by his bed, staring down. The other was on the other side of the bars, holding a rifle. Both could not have looked more serious.

"You ready to travel, boy?" the Pinkerton in the cell asked.

Shiloh opened his eyes slowly. "That depends. No man wants a trip to his own hanging."

"This is a trip on the railroad," the one outside the bars answered. "Courtesy of Allan Pinkerton and the Pinkerton Agency, but you say that to anyone, and I'll call you a liar."

Shiloh made to rise up off the bunk. "What about that dead man? You saying that you believe me when I say he killed Brady?"

"Son, I wouldn't believe you if you said dogs got four legs," the Pinkerton in the cell replied. His face was bent into an attitude of complete and utter disgust.

Shiloh tested his legs on the floor; they weren't sturdy, but they'd do. "Then hang me," he said.

"Fact is, he did kill Chris Brady. We found a watch with Brady's name in it in his saddlebag. That fat one you killed a ways back, he had enough of the wife's geegaws, rings and alike, to hang *him*. You just got lucky."

Shiloh tried to walk, took a step, thought better of it, and sat back down.

"You listening, boy?" the one outside the bars put in. "That sheriff you killed, he was kin to them."

"Kin?" Shiloh asked. "It wasn't me that killed him."

The Pinkerton in the cage smiled at this. "You going to deny it after I tell you he's worth two hundred dollars to the man who did? Seems that before he turned to sheriffing, he tossed a wide rope up near Fernley. You want to hear 'bout how he killed a rancher up there?"

Shiloh didn't answer; he was waiting for the pain in his head to pass. Bringing a hand around the back, he could feel where the pick handle had laid him out.

"Maybe you want to hear 'bout how he was bleeding this town dry?"

"You figure it's too much bother to get some clothes?" Shiloh asked.

"Hell no," the one outside said, then slipped a complete set, brand new, through the bars. "These come out of the two hundred, plus the five hundred for the two men."

The Pink inside took the clothes and tossed them on the bunk. "Now, this is the way it's gonna be," he said. "The train pulls in in about an hour. You're gonna be on it."

"That's the way it's going to be?" Shiloh asked, trying to slip his feet into the long suit. "They had my money, almost five thousand in gold."

"Awful lot of money," the one in the cage said. "Awful lot of money."

"We're wasting time," the other answered. Shiloh stared mute as the Pink snapped open a gold pocket watch that looked brand new.

"Only money we know about is the reward for them two. Appears they wired the reward money down to Texas," the one with the rifle said. "A mistake, like."

"There's another way it could be," the other Pink said, snapping the watch shut. "You so much as look cross-eyed at anyone, you kill a damn fly, any time between now and when you step on that train, I'll put a bullet in your back."

Shiloh had put his pants on, and was working to get into the blue wool shirt. "I need to head up near Copley again," he said.

The Pinkerton in the cell chuckled. "You hear that? This ole boy, he wants to take a train ride to Copley."

"Shit, Copley," the Pinkerton with the rifle spat. "There ain't nothing for you in Copley 'cept a young hot-head with one foot, swearing he's gonna blow your head off next time he sees you."

Shiloh picked up his blue Union jacket. Someone had cleaned, brushed, and mended it. When he spoke again, it was almost in a whisper. "Need to see where they buried Chris and his wife."

"They're buried proper," the man closest said. "Not in town. Out near his spread."

"Out near his spread," Shiloh repeated.

"They'll be smelling wildflowers and juniper on Judgment Day."

Shiloh was sitting on the bunk, jacket in his lap, trying to see in his head two graves with neat white markers in a field of flowers.

The Pinkerton with the rifle came in close to the bars then. "What was he to you, anyway?"

GILES TIPPETTE

Author of the best-selling WILSON YOUNG
SERIES, BAD NEWS, and CROSS FIRE
is back with his most exciting
Western adventure yet!

JAILBREAK

Time is running out for Justa Williams, owner of the Half-
Moon Ranch in West Texas. His brother Norris is being
held in a Mexican jail, and neither bribes nor threats can
free him.

Now, with the help of a dozen kill-crazy Mexican *banditos*,
Justa aims to blast Norris out. But the worst is yet to come:
a hundred-mile chase across the Mexican desert with fifty
federales in hot pursuit.

The odds of reaching the Texas border are a million to nothing . . . and if the Williams brothers don't watch their backs,
the road to freedom could turn into the road to hell!

JAILBREAK
by
Giles Tippette

On sale now, wherever Jove Books are sold!

*Turn the page for a sample of
this exciting new Western*

1

AT SUPPER NORRIS, my middle brother, said, "I think we got some trouble on that five thousand acres down on the border near Laredo."

He said it serious, which is the way Norris generally says everything. I quit wrestling with the steak Buttercup, our cook, had turned into rawhide and said, "What are you talking about? How could we have trouble on land lying idle?"

He said, "I got word from town this afternoon that a telegram had come in from a friend of ours down there. He says we got some kind of squatters taking up residence on the place."

My youngest brother, Ben, put his fork down and said, incredulously, "*That* five thousand acres? Hell, it ain't nothing but rocks and cactus and sand. Why in hell would anyone want to squat on that worthless piece of nothing?"

Norris just shook his head. "I don't know. But that's what the telegram said. Came from Jack Cole. And if anyone ought to know what's going on down there it would be him."

I thought about it and it didn't make a bit of sense. I was Justa Williams, and my family, my two brothers and myself and our father, Howard, occupied a considerable ranch called the Half-Moon down along the Gulf of Mexico in Matagorda County, Texas. It was some of the best grazing land in the state and we had one of the best herds of purebred and crossbred cattle in that part of the country. In short we were pretty well-to-do.

But that didn't make us any the less ready to be stolen from, if indeed that was the case. The five thousand acres Norris had been talking about had come to us through a trade our father had made some years before. We'd never made any use of the land, mainly because, as Ben had said, it was pretty worthless and because it was a good two hundred miles from our ranch headquarters. On a few occasions we'd bought cattle in Mexico and then used the acreage to hold small groups on while we made up a herd. But other than that, it lay mainly forgotten.

I frowned. "Norris, this doesn't make a damn bit of sense. Right after supper send a man into Blessing with a return wire for Jack asking him if he's certain. What the hell kind of squatting could anybody be doing on that land?"

Ben said, "Maybe they're raisin' watermelons." He laughed.

I said, "They could raise melons, but there damn sure wouldn't be no water in them."

Norris said, "Well, it bears looking into." He got up, throwing his napkin on the table. "I'll go write out that telegram."

I watched him go, dressed, as always, in his town clothes. Norris was the businessman in the family. He'd been sent down to the University at Austin and had got considerable learning about the ins and outs of banking and land deals and all the other parts of our business that didn't directly involve the ranch. At the age of twenty-nine I'd been the boss of the operation a good deal longer than I cared to think about. It had been thrust upon me by our father when I wasn't much more than twenty. He'd said he'd wanted me to take over while he was still strong enough to help me out of my mistakes and I reckoned that was partly true. But it had just seemed that after our mother had died the life had sort of gone out of him. He'd been one of the earliest settlers, taking up the land not long after Texas had become a republic in 1845. I figured all the years of fighting Indians and then Yankees and scalawags and carpetbaggers and cattle thieves had taken their toll on him. Then a few years back he'd been nicked in the lungs by a bullet that should never have been allowed to head his way and it had thrown an extra strain on his heart. He was pushing seventy and he still had plenty of head on his shoulders, but mostly all he did now was sit around in his rocking chair and stare out over the cattle and land business he'd built. Not to say that I didn't go to him for advice when the occasion demanded. I did, and mostly I took it.

Buttercup came in just then and sat down at the end of the table with a cup of coffee. He was near as old as Dad and almost completely worthless. But he'd been one of the first hands that Dad had hired and he'd been kept on even after he couldn't sit a horse anymore. The problem was he'd elected himself cook, and that was the sorriest day our family had ever seen. There were two Mexican women hired to cook for the twelve riders we kept full time, but Buttercup insisted on cooking for the family.

Mainly, I think, because he thought he was one of the family. A notion we could never completely dissuade him from.

So he sat there, about two days of stubble on his face, looking as scrawny as a pecked-out rooster, sweat running down his face, his apron a mess. He said, wiping his forearm across his forehead, "Boy, it shore be hot in there. You boys shore better be glad you ain't got no business takes you in that kitchen."

Ben said, in a loud mutter, "I wish you didn't either."

Ben, at twenty-five, was easily the best man with a horse or a gun that I had ever seen. His only drawback was that he was hotheaded and he tended to act first and think later. That ain't a real good combination for someone that could go on the prod as fast as Ben. When I had argued with Dad about taking over as boss, suggesting instead that Norris, with his education, was a much better choice, Dad had simply said, "Yes, in some ways. But he can't handle Ben. You can. You can handle Norris, too. But none of them can handle you."

Well, that hadn't been exactly true. If Dad had wished it I would have taken orders from Norris even though he was two years younger than me. But the logic in Dad's line of thinking had been that the Half-Moon and our cattle business was the lodestone of all our businesses and only I could run that. He had been right. In the past I'd imported purebred Whiteface and Hereford cattle from up North, bred them to our native Longhorns and produced cattle that would bring twice as much at market as the horse-killing, all-bone, all-wild Longhorns. My neighbors had laughed at me at first, claiming those square little purebreds would never make it in our Texas heat. But they'd been wrong and, one by one, they'd followed the example of the Half-Moon.

Buttercup was setting up to take off on another one of his long-winded harangues about how it had been in the "old days" so I quickly got up, excusing myself, and went into the big office we used for sitting around in as well as a place of business. Norris was at the desk composing his telegram so I poured myself out a whiskey and sat down. I didn't want to hear about any trouble over some worthless five thousand acres of borderland. In fact I didn't want to hear about any troubles of any kind. I was just two weeks short of getting married, married to a lady I'd been courting off and on for five years, and I was mighty anxious that nothing come up to interfere with our plans. Her name was Nora Parker and her daddy owned and run the general mercantile in our nearest town, Blessing. I'd almost lost her once before to a Kansas City drummer. She'd finally gotten tired of waiting on me, waiting until the ranch didn't occupy all my time, and almost run off with a smooth-talking Kansas City drummer that called on her daddy in the harness trade. But she'd come to her senses in time and got off the train in Texarkana and returned home.

But even then it had been a close thing. I, along with my men and brothers and help from some of our neighbors, had been involved with stopping a huge herd of illegal cattle being driven up from Mexico from crossing our range and infecting our cattle with tick fever which could have wiped us all out. I tell you it had been a bloody business. We'd lost four good men and had to kill at least a half dozen on the other side. Fact of the business was I'd come about as close as I ever had to getting killed myself, and that was going some for the sort of rough-and-tumble life I'd led.

Nora had almost quit me over it, saying she just couldn't take the uncertainty. But in the end, she'd stuck by me. That had been the year before, 1896, and I'd convinced her that civilized law was coming to the country, but until it did, we that had been there before might have to take things into our own hands from time to time.

She'd seen that and had understood. I loved her and she loved me and that was enough to overcome any of the troubles we were still likely to encounter from day to day.

So I was giving Norris a pretty sour look as he finished his telegram and sent for a hired hand to ride it into Blessing, seven miles away. I said, "Norris, let's don't make a big fuss about this. That land ain't even crossed my mind in at least a couple of years. Likely we got a few Mexican families squatting down there and trying to scratch out a few acres of corn."

Norris gave me his businessman's look. He said, "It's our land, Justa. And if we allow anyone to squat on it for long enough or put up a fence they can lay claim. That's the law. My job is to see that we protect what we have, not give it away."

I sipped at my whiskey and studied Norris. In his town clothes he didn't look very impressive. He'd inherited more from our mother than from Dad so he was not as wide-shouldered and slim-hipped as Ben and me. But I knew him to be a good, strong, dependable man in any kind of fight. Of course he wasn't that good with a gun, but then Ben and I weren't all that good with books like he was. But I said, just to jolly him a bit, "Norris, I do believe you are running to suet. I may have to put you out with Ben working the horse herd and work a little of that fat off you."

Naturally it got his goat. Norris had always envied Ben and me a little. I was just over six foot and weighed right around a hundred and ninety. I had inherited my daddy's big hands and big shoulders. Ben was almost a copy of me except he was about a size smaller. Norris said, "I weigh the same as I have for the last five years. If it's any of your business."

I said, as if I was being serious, "Must be them sack suits you wear. What they do, pad them around the middle?"

He said, "Why don't you just go to hell."

After he'd stomped out of the room I got the bottle of whiskey and an extra glass and went down to Dad's room. It had been one of his bad days and he'd taken to bed right after lunch. Strictly speaking he wasn't supposed to have no whiskey, but I watered him down a shot every now and then and it didn't seem to do him no harm.

He was sitting up when I came in the room. I took a moment to fix him a little drink, using some water out of his pitcher, then handed him the glass and sat down in the easy chair by the bed. I told him what Norris had reported and asked what he thought.

He took a sip of his drink and shook his head. "Beats all I ever heard," he said. "I took that land in trade for a bad debt some fifteen, twenty years ago. I reckon I'd of been money ahead if I'd of hung on to the bad debt. That land won't even raise weeds, well as I remember, and Noah was in on the last rain that fell on the place."

We had considerable amounts of land spotted around the state as a result of this kind of trade or that. It was Norris's business to keep up with their management. I was just bringing this to Dad's attention more out of boredom and impatience for my wedding day to arrive than anything else.

I said, "Well, it's a mystery to me. How you feeling?"

He half smiled. "Old." Then he looked into his glass. "And I never liked watered whiskey. Pour me a dollop of the straight stuff in here."

I said, "Now, Howard. You know—"

He cut me off. "If I wanted somebody to argue with I'd send for Buttercup. Now do like I told you."

I did, but I felt guilty about it. He took the slug of whiskey down in one pull. Then he leaned his head back on the pillow and said, "Aaaaah. I don't give a damn what that horse doctor says, ain't nothing makes a man feel as good inside as a shot of the best."

I felt sorry for him laying there. He'd always led just the kind of life he wanted—going where he wanted, doing what he wanted, having what he set out to get. And now he was reduced to being a semi-invalid. But one thing that showed the strength that was still in him was that you *never* heard him complain. He said, "How's the cattle?"

I said, "They're doing all right, but I tell you we could do with a little of Noah's flood right now. All this heat and no rain is curing the grass off way ahead of time. If it doesn't let up we'll be feeding hay by late September, early October. And that will play hell on our supply. Could be we won't have enough to last through the winter. Norris thinks we ought to sell off five hundred herd or so, but the market is doing poorly right now. I'd rather chance the weather than take a sure beating by selling off."

He sort of shrugged and closed his eyes. The whiskey was relaxing him. He said, "You're the boss."

"Yeah," I said. "Damn my luck."

I wandered out of the back of the house. Even though it was nearing seven o'clock of the evening it was still good and hot. Off in the distance, about a half a mile away, I could see the outline of the house I was building for Nora and myself. It was going to be a close thing to get it finished by our wedding day. Not having any riders to spare for the project, I'd imported a building contractor from Galveston, sixty miles away. He'd arrived with a half a dozen Mexican laborers and a few skilled masons and they'd set up a little tent city around the place. The contractor had gone back to Galveston to fetch some materials, leaving his Mexicans behind. I walked along idly, hoping he wouldn't forget that the job wasn't done. He had some of my money, but not near what he'd get when he finished the job.

Just then Ray Hays came hurrying across the back lot toward me. Ray was kind of a special case for me. The only problem with that was that he knew it and wasn't a bit above taking advantage of the situation. Once, a few years past, he'd saved my life by going against an evil man that he was working for at the time, an evil man who meant to have my life. In gratitude I'd given Ray a good job at the Half-Moon, letting him work directly under Ben, who was responsible for the horse herd. He was a good, steady man and a good man with a gun. He was also fair company. When he wasn't talking.

He came churning up to me, mopping his brow. He said, "Lordy, boss, it is—"

I said, "Hays, if you say it's hot I'm going to knock you down."

He gave me a look that was a mixture of astonishment and hurt. He said, "Why, whatever for?"

I said, "*Everybody* knows it's hot. Does every son of a bitch you run into have to make mention of the fact?"

His brow furrowed. "Well, I never thought of it that way. I 'spect you are right. Goin' down to look at yore house?"

I shook my head. "No. It makes me nervous to see how far they've got to go. I can't see any way it'll be ready on time."

He said, "Miss Nora ain't gonna like that."

I gave him a look. "I guess you felt forced to say that."

He looked down. "Well, maybe she won't mind."

I said, grimly, "The hell she won't. She'll think I did it a-purpose."

"Aw, she wouldn't."

"Naturally you know so much about it, Hays. Why don't you tell me a few other things about her."

"I was jest tryin' to lift yore spirits, boss."

I said, "You keep trying to lift my spirits and I'll put you on the haying crew."

He looked horrified. No real cowhand wanted any work he couldn't do from the back of his horse. Haying was a hot, hard, sweaty job done either afoot or from a wagon seat. We generally brought in contract Mexican labor to handle ours. But I'd been known in the past to discipline a cowhand by giving him a few days on the hay gang. Hays said, "Boss, now I never meant nothin'. I swear. You know me, my mouth gets to runnin' sometimes. I swear I'm gonna watch it."

I smiled. Hays always made me smile. He was so easily buffaloed. He had it soft at the Half-Moon and he knew it and didn't want to take any chances on losing a good thing.

I lit up a cigarillo and watched dusk settle in over the coastal plains. It wasn't but three miles to Matagorda Bay and it was quiet enough I felt like I could almost hear the waves breaking on the shore. Somewhere in the distance a mama cow bawled for her calf. The spring crop were near about weaned by now, but there were still a few mamas that wouldn't cut the apron strings. I stood there reflecting on how peaceful things had been of late. It suited me just fine. All I wanted was to get my house finished, marry Nora and never handle another gun so long as I lived.

The peace and quiet were short-lived. Within twenty-four hours we'd had a return telegram from Jack Cole. It said:

YOUR LAND OCCUPIED BY TEN MEN TO TWELVE MEN STOP CAN'T BE SURE WHAT THEY'RE DOING BECAUSE THEY RUN STRANGERS OFF STOP APPEAR TO HAVE A GOOD MANY CATTLE GATHERED STOP APPEAR TO BE FENCING STOP ALL I KNOW STOP

I read the telegram twice and then I said, "Why this is crazy as hell! That land wouldn't support fifty head of cattle."

We were all gathered in the big office. Even Dad was there, sitting in his rocking chair. I looked up at him. "What do you make of this, Howard?"

He shook his big, old head of white hair. "Beats the hell out of me, Justa. I can't figure it."

Ben said, "Well, I don't see where it has to be figured. I'll take five men and go down there and run them off. I don't care what they're doing. They ain't got no business on our land."

I said, "Take it easy, Ben. Aside from the fact you don't need to be getting into any more fights this year, I can't spare you or five men. The way this grass is drying up we've got to keep drifting those cattle."

Norris said, "No, Ben is right. We can't have such affairs going on with our property. But we'll handle it within the law. I'll simply take the train down there, hire a good lawyer and have the matter settled by the sheriff. Shouldn't take but a few days."

Well, there wasn't much I could say to that. We couldn't very well let people take advantage of us, but I still hated to be without Norris's services even for a few days. On matters other than the ranch he was the expert, and it didn't seem like there was a day went by that some financial question didn't come up that only he could answer. I said, "Are you sure you can spare yourself for a few days?"

He thought for a moment and then nodded. "I don't see why not. I've just moved most of our available cash into short-term municipal bonds in Galveston. The market is looking all right and everything appears fine at the bank. I can't think of anything that might come up."

I said, "All right. But you just keep this in mind. You are not a gun hand. You are not a fighter. I do not want you going anywhere near those people, whoever they are. You do it legal and let the sheriff handle the eviction. Is that understood?"

He kind of swelled up, resenting the implication that he couldn't handle himself. The biggest trouble I'd had through the years when trouble had come up had been keeping Norris out of it. Why he couldn't just be content to be a wagon load of brains was more than I could understand. He said, "Didn't you just hear me say I intended to go through a lawyer and the sheriff? Didn't I just say that?"

I said, "I wanted to be sure you heard yourself."

He said, "Nothing wrong with my hearing. Nor my approach to this matter. You seem to constantly be taken with the idea that I'm always looking for a fight. I think you've got the wrong brother. I use logic."

"Yeah?" I said. "You remember when that guy kicked you in the balls when they were holding guns on us? And then we chased them twenty miles and finally caught them?"

He looked away. "That has nothing to do with this."

"Yeah?" I said, enjoying myself. "And here's this guy, shot all to hell. And what was it you insisted on doing?"

Ben laughed, but Norris wouldn't say anything.

I said, "Didn't you insist on us standing him up so you could kick him in the balls? Didn't you?"

He sort of growled, "Oh, go to hell."

I said, "I just want to know where the logic was in that."

He said, "Right is right. I was simply paying him back in kind. It was the only thing his kind could understand."

I said, "That's my point. You just don't go down there and go to paying back a bunch of rough hombres in kind. Or any other currency for that matter."

That made him look over at Dad. He said, "Dad, will you make him quit treating me like I was ten years old? He does it on purpose."

But he'd appealed to the wrong man. Dad just threw his hands in the air and said, "Don't come to me with your troubles. I'm just a boarder around here. You get your orders from Justa. You know that."

Of course he didn't like that. Norris had always been a strong hand for the right and wrong of a matter. In fact, he may have been one of the most stubborn men I'd ever met. But he didn't say anything, just gave me a look and muttered something about hoping a mess came up at the bank while I was gone and then see how much boss I was.

But he didn't mean nothing by it. Like most families, we fought amongst ourselves and, like most families, God help the outsider who tried to interfere with one of us.

A special offer for people who enjoy reading the best Westerns published today. If you enjoyed this book, subscribe now and get . . .

TWO FREE WESTERNS!
A $5.90 VALUE—NO OBLIGATION

If you enjoyed this book and would like to read more of the very best Westerns being published today, you'll want to subscribe to True Value's Western Home Subscription Service. If you enjoyed the book you just read and want more of the most exciting, adventurous, action packed Westerns, subscribe now.

TWO FREE BOOKS

When you subscribe, we'll send you your first month's shipment of the newest and best 6 Westerns for you to preview. With your first shipment, two of these books will be yours as our introductory gift to you absolutely FREE, regardless of what you decide to do.

Special Subscriber Savings

As a True Value subscriber all regular monthly selections will be billed at the low subscriber price of just $2.45 each. That's at least a savings of $3.00 each month below the publishers price. There is never any shipping, handling or other hidden charges. What's more there is no minimum number of books you must buy, you may return any selection for full credit and you can cancel your subscription at any time. A TRUE VALUE!

～ Mail the coupon below ～

To start your subscription and receive 2 FREE WESTERNS, fill out the coupon below and mail it today. We'll send your first shipment which includes 2 FREE BOOKS as soon as we receive it.